THE DARK CARD

Laura is hiding. Numb from her mother's recent death, she is staying alone in her family's house by the Jersey Shore, barely managing to get through the days. It's only through Billy, an Atlantic City blackjack dealer, that she begins to come alive. His stories of the glamour and glitter of the casinos draw her in, and soon she is putting on her mother's jewelry and makeup, creating a false identity that allows her to gamble there herself. The risk and danger escalate when she meets Ari Hassan, a professional gambler whose stakes are higher than money. And the more time Laura spends with him, the less chance she has of beating the odds . . . and coming out alive.

"The author has created [a novel of] suspense and excitement." —*Voice of Youth Advocates*

"Even minor characters here are well-drawn, while relationships are deftly portrayed. Ari and the gaming table provide enough potential menace to keep the suspense taut. . . . Thoughtfully explores the complicated feelings that can follow the loss of a flawed parent." —*Kirkus Reviews*

D1274996

AMY EHRLICH

THE DARK CARD

PUFFIN BOOKS

PUFFIN BOOKS
Published by the Penguin Group
Penguin Books USA Inc., 375 Hudson Street, New York, New York 10014, U.S.A.
Penguin Books Ltd, 27 Wrights Lane, London W8 5TZ, England
Penguin Books Australia Ltd, Ringwood, Victoria, Australia
Penguin Books Canada Ltd, 10 Alcorn Avenue, Toronto, Ontario, Canada M4V 3B2
Penguin Books (N.Z.) Ltd, 182–190 Wairau Road, Auckland 10, New Zealand

Penguin Books Ltd, Registered Offices: Harmondsworth, Middlesex, England

First published in the United States of America by Viking Penguin,
a division of Penguin Books USA Inc., 1991
Published in Puffin Books, 1993

1 3 5 7 9 10 8 6 4 2

LIBRARY OF CONGRESS CATALOGING-IN-PUBLICATION DATA
Ehrlich, Amy, 1942–
The dark card / Amy Ehrlich.   p.   cm.
Summary: While trying to come to terms with her mother's death,
Laura is lured by the glamour and anonymity of Atlantic City's
casinos, where she uses her mother's jewelry and makeup to create a new identity for herself.
ISBN 0-14-036332-7
[1. Atlantic City (N.J.)—Fiction.   2. Death—Fiction.   3. Mothers
and daughters—Fiction.]   I. Title.
PZ7.E328Dar 1993   [Fic]—dc20   92-37576

Printed in the United States of America
Set in Electra

for

RUTH HORNBEIN

and with thanks to

DAVID INGRAHAM

THE DARK CARD

CHAPTER
1

The furniture in the living room looked to Laura like a collection of ghosts. The sofas and chairs were covered with sheets and the green brocade drapes were drawn. It was two in the afternoon, but Laura had just gotten up. She was alone in the house.

All weekend she and her father had hardly said a word to each other. They'd fixed their own food, and in the evening, after it got dark, they'd sat out on the screened porch with the television set on. But on Sunday night, just before the taxi came to pick him up, Laura's father asked her if she was sure she wanted to stay in Ventnor.

"Look," Laura had answered, "I'm seventeen years old and you said I could stay here. You promised."

Then he'd shrugged and kissed her on the cheek and nodded to the driver to get going.

The house in Ventnor belonged to her Philadelphia grandparents, but they were too old to use it now. It was a white stucco house with a green tile roof and it was just south of Atlantic City, half a block from the ocean. Every summer since Laura could remember, she and her older sister, Heather, and their mother had packed up their big station wagon the day after school ended and driven down to Ventnor from Manhattan. Her father came only on weekends, but the three of them stayed all summer long, right through to Labor Day.

In the winter the house was boarded up; nobody used it. Once last January she'd driven down with a boy she'd been seeing, a college boy named Joseph, and broken in through the coal chute in the basement. They'd drunk her father's liquor but left everything else alone. She didn't want to get caught. She felt as if she was trespassing. The sheets had been on the furniture then, too, she remembered.

Laura wandered into the kitchen and took two doughnuts out of a box in the refrigerator. Then she went back to the living room and sat down on one of the ghostly sofas. The air conditioner was on and it made her flesh cold, but Laura sat in her cotton nightgown, slowly eating doughnuts, forcing herself to chew and swallow.

All her natural rhythms of eating and sleeping had been disturbed. She couldn't eat meat anymore, or fish or chicken or eggs. Whenever she tried to, she would retch. Her mother had died on May 4th, in Mount Sinai Hospital in Manhattan, of a kind of cancer called lymphoma, and it had had many strange effects on Laura.

Every night for nine months, since she'd known about her mother's illness, known she was going to die, Laura had slept as if a shroud were over her, deep and heavy, pressing her to her bed. Her dreams were terrifying, though she could never remember them, and in the morning her body ached so much she could hardly move.

Laura had thought that once she was in Ventnor, all the accumulated weight of that time would evaporate into the glittering sea air. She pictured herself eating big meals again and getting up at sunrise. But instead, for three days she'd eaten nothing but fruit yogurt and doughnuts, and she'd slept until two in the afternoon. She felt as if she were still asleep now.

When the doorbell rang, it took her by surprise. At first she wasn't even sure what it was. But whoever was there kept ringing it, and finally Laura pulled herself off the sofa and went to the door.

The light outside was blinding. The person who stood in the doorway was at first completely blotted out by the brilliant white light of the sky, and then Laura realized it was Gabrielle, her best friend in Ventnor since they were five.

"Laura!" cried Gabrielle. She looked frightened. They had not spoken to each other since Laura's mother died.

Gabrielle's curly brown hair was different, longer, and her face had changed, too, but Laura recognized the bathing suit she was wearing from last summer. It was a purple two-

3

piece suit and Gabrielle's body in contrast seemed unusually white.

"You look the same. A little thinner, maybe," said Gabrielle. "I was afraid you'd be different."

"I am different," Laura said, pulling her inside and closing the door. "What did you think?"

Gabrielle's eyes darted around the room. "Isn't your father here?"

"No, he left last night. He'll be down only on weekends, the same as before."

"He'll let you stay alone during the week?"

"It's safer for me here than in New York," said Laura. "Nothing can happen. Besides Heather will be coming next week."

"That's good," said Gabrielle. "I'm going to be really busy. I have a job now. I'm working." She didn't look at Laura.

"Doing what?"

"My mother got me a job in the kitchens at Claridge's. I work the evening shift, from two until ten, but I got someone to change with me today so I could see you.

"Three of us are working in A.C. now. Me, my mom, and Billy. He went to dealer school last winter and now he's dealing blackjack at Trump Plaza. Did I tell you? It's really funny. You know how my dad feels about the casinos. He's so religious, he thinks they're sinful. But they pay so well that what can he do?"

Laura was silent. She thought of her own summer stretching ahead endlessly, of nights and days still to come. She'd been counting on hanging around with Gabrielle and Gabrielle's friends from Holy Spirit High School the way she had last year, but the others probably had casino jobs by now, too.

Gabrielle sat down in a big wing chair. "My mother said you could come over to our house whenever you wanted. She told me to tell you that."

Something in Gabrielle's manner was getting to Laura. "That's okay, you don't have to feel sorry for me. I can take care of myself," she said shortly.

"I just want to be your friend, Laura. This is so weird for me. . . ."

"What about me?" said Laura. "How do you think it is for me?" She knew she was going to make Gabrielle miserable, but she couldn't stop herself and she didn't care. "It's my mother who died, not yours. And you never even called me all winter. Did you think I didn't notice that?"

Gabrielle shifted and hunched in the wing chair. Her white skin seemed to glisten. "God, Laura, I'm sorry. I tried to write you, but I never could. I must have ripped up twelve letters.

"My mother said I should think of something good to say about your mother, a good memory you could treasure, but you know me. All I could think of was that time last August when she dressed up as a vampire for the Batchelders' costume party. I keep seeing her in her dressing room, putting straws on her teeth for fangs. She was so interesting, your mother. I can't believe she's dead. How could she be?"

"Cancer moves fast," said Laura. The truth was that she'd forgotten this memory of Gabrielle's and it bothered her. Why had her mother dressed as a vampire? In August her neck had already begun to swell on the left side, but they thought it was an abscessed tooth. The diagnosis of lymphoma had come when they were back in New York, over Labor Day weekend.

Don't think of it, Laura warned herself as the images began to roll across her mind. Gabrielle would never have these images. She would never need to see Laura's mother getting thinner and thinner until she looked like a paper-doll cutout in the white hospital bed. She'd never need to hear her coughing at night as her lungs filled with fluid or see her head bald from radiation.

"Look, Gabrielle. I really don't want to talk about it. Forget what I said about not calling. I don't know what I'm saying half the time lately."

"That's okay," said Gabrielle. "It's not your fault."

Laura walked to the front of the room and pulled on the metal bar that opened the drapes. They swung apart wildly and the room flooded with light. In the sunshine, dust swirled everywhere.

"Don't you want to go to the beach?" Gabrielle stared out the window. "It's a great beach day. Hot with a wind."

"I guess," said Laura and went upstairs to change into her bathing suit. Gabrielle had taken the afternoon off from work and had come to see her. Going to the beach with Gabrielle was the least she could do.

Light glared from the asphalt of Marion Avenue and from the white sand on the other side of the boardwalk. Laura and Gabrielle walked down to the water's edge, and set up their red-and-white-striped beach chairs near the tideline.

6

Laura closed her eyes. She liked the hot sun beating down and the way the sounds on the beach were muted and distant, but Gabrielle wanted to talk.

"Remember Greg Wilkins? We used to see him surfing at the Ventnor Pier? He went to Atlantic City High School, so even though he's really cute, I never thought I'd meet him. But then in February Susan Lacroix had a party.

"Laura, he came right over to me and these were his exact words, I swear it: 'You look as good in that sweater as you did in your purple bathing suit last summer.' God, I couldn't believe it! We've been going out every weekend since. He's really nice, much more serious than you'd think. He's even talking about getting married when I graduate, but I told him we were too young for that."

"How old is he?" Laura tried to remember Greg, but could picture only a swarthy, thickset boy in a wetsuit.

"Twenty. He's working in A.C., too, as a security guard at Showboat. The pay is really good. He makes nine dollars an hour."

It was quiet and Laura thought Gabrielle had finished, but then she said, "What about you? Did you meet anyone over the winter? I hope this doesn't sound weird because of your mother, but it's possible, right? You can never tell."

"Well, actually I did." Laura adjusted the back of her chair so that she could lie flat. "His name was Joseph. He went to Columbia."

"What's that?"

"Columbia University. It's in Manhattan."

"I never heard of it," said Gabrielle. "Go on."

"There's not much to tell. We're not seeing each other anymore. He was good for a while, he kept my mind off things. He had a nice car."

"Laura! What a thing to say!"

"But it's the truth," said Laura. Joseph's car had been a red Scout with a high front window and a great sound system. He loved to drive. He'd pick Laura up from the hospital every night at seven and they'd head out of Manhattan, traveling fast. Sometimes they went to Long Island or Connecticut. That one time they went all the way to Ventnor.

Joseph smoked dope but Laura never wanted any. For her it was enough just to be driving. She liked to have the heater on and the windows rolled down even on the coldest nights. She felt peaceful then, and all the turmoil and pain of her hours in the hospital would disappear.

That's what she needed right now, Laura suddenly decided, some kind of pure feeling to blot out everything else.

Without saying anything to Gabrielle, she threw herself into the ocean. Thousands of pale bubbles surrounded her and her eyes stung from the salt. She swam hard until she'd gone well beyond the breakers. Once she looked back to shore and was startled at how tiny the umbrellas and people seemed. But that was always true, she told herself; things always appeared farther away than they were.

A lifeguard stood up and blew his whistle, but Laura ignored it. They wouldn't come after her unless she were in danger, and Laura knew she was perfectly safe. Her body lay on the ocean swells, bobbing slowly up and down. No thoughts were in her mind, only the vast blue sky above her.

"You deaf or something? What's the matter with you?" someone screamed. Hands reached out for her, slipping along her ribs and holding fast.

Laura's head went under and she gagged as saltwater filled her mouth and nostrils. She couldn't move or breathe. She felt as if she were drowning. Then suddenly she was being hauled into a lifeboat. It rocked crazily and nearly capsized. Laura and the two lifeguards who'd rescued her glared at each other.

"Look what you did to me!" she cried. Blood oozed from two long scrapes on the front of her legs where they'd pulled her up the side of the boat.

"So sue us," said one of the lifeguards. "Be my guest. You're lucky to be alive."

"I was fine out there. I'm a good swimmer."

"Yeah, sure. You were drifting away, that's all. The undertow out there was carrying you off."

"You don't have to yell at me," Laura said.

A crowd had gathered on the beach. Mothers held their children tightly by the hands and old people in beach hats and sunglasses whispered to each other. Nobody moved forward to help as the lifeguards jumped into the shallow waves and pulled the boat up. But afterward there was scattered clapping, applause for the lifeguards' bravery.

Laura sat alone in the boat waiting to see what would happen. She was suddenly unbearably cold and her teeth chattered. She felt like a criminal. One of the lifeguards appeared at the side of the boat with a clipboard. "I'll need to get some information from you," he said. "To file a report."

Laura told him her address and phone number in Ventnor, but said she was eighteen, not seventeen. She hoped that meant they wouldn't notify her father. She didn't want her father to find out.

"You can go," the lifeguard said, as she continued to sit there. "Did you come to the beach with anyone?"

"Yes, me," said Gabrielle. She pushed forward, holding Laura's towel. "Here, take this," she told Laura.

Without a word, the two of them gathered their things and walked to the boardwalk. "Let's sit here for a while," Laura said, leaning her beach chair against a silvery wooden bench. "I don't want to go home yet."

"Are you all right?"

"Sure. You didn't think I was drowning, did you?"

Gabrielle shook her head. "Not really. But why didn't you come in when he blew the whistle?"

"It was so nice out there. I felt like being alone."

"You mean you wanted to get away from me?" Gabrielle had her sunglasses on, but Laura could still see that she was upset.

"It's hard to explain. It's not really you. But sometimes everything that anyone says sounds like a foreign language. It doesn't make any sense, you know? Like when you were talking about your boyfriend, all I could think was that a hurricane could come in from the ocean and blow down Ventnor. Then what difference would it make if you had a boyfriend or not?"

Gabrielle jumped up. "That's an awful thing to say! I don't understand. Why are you being so mean?"

"I told you it wasn't you, Gabrielle. You take things too personally."

All she had to do, Laura knew, was to put her arms around her friend and explain the way that death was always in her thoughts now, undermining everything. If she explained it carefully, she could make Gabrielle understand. But Laura was too tired for that.

So she stayed on the beach and watched as Gabrielle ran away, barefoot down the boardwalk. The blood dried on the scrapes on her legs and the sun moved slowly across the sky, turning her skin pink, but Laura hardly noticed.

CHAPTER
2

She thought that Gabrielle would call her. After all, she reasoned, it was Gabrielle who'd gotten mad, Gabrielle who'd run away. But the phone never rang in the empty house, except at eight at night and then it was her father, checking up on her. "I'm fine," Laura told him. "I've been going to the beach with Gabrielle every day. We're going to the movies in Margate tonight with some other girls."

Actually she did try calling two of Gabrielle's friends, girls who had always acted interested in her, but they were both busy, either working or gone. Her father and Heather would be coming Friday night, but on Thursday morning when Laura woke up and looked in the bathroom mirror, she knew she had to find someone to talk to right away.

She recognized herself, of course. It wasn't that. But her face had no meaning for her. It just hung there in the mirror, smiling at her when she smiled and blinking when she blinked. Finally Laura had to look away, just to separate herself from that other face.

In a panic she got out of her nightgown and turned the shower on as hot as she could stand. It rained down on her, searing her shoulders with heat. Laura washed her hair and shaved her legs and under her arms. She'd decided to go next door to Gabrielle's and apologize, and it seemed important to look good.

Instead of shorts and a T-shirt, she chose a black cotton sundress to wear. Not for mourning, she hoped the Ruzzos wouldn't think that, but because it was comfortable and cool, and their house wasn't air-conditioned.

Ever since Laura had known the Ruzzos, they had fascinated her. In a way, she liked the idea of them, of the entire family, better than she liked Gabrielle. There was always something going on in their house, a party or a celebration of some kind. Nothing pleased Mrs. Ruzzo more than to have all her relatives around the table. Her children's friends were counted as relatives, too, that was the best part.

There were three children in the family. Gabrielle's sister Marna had been a friend of Heather's for a while, but she was married now and lived offshore, somewhere near Camden. Billy Ruzzo, Gabrielle's older brother, was more of a mystery to Laura. When she and Gabrielle were fourteen, he'd left college and joined the merchant marines, and she hadn't seen him since.

13

But that Thursday morning it was Billy who let Laura into the Ruzzos' kitchen. Rock and roll music was playing, but nobody else seemed to be home. He grinned at her and crossed his arms in a languid way. "Aren't you going to sit down?" he said.

The kitchen looked just the way she remembered it, with gauzy yellow curtains over the sink, and the linoleum floor waxed and shiny. Billy must have been eating his lunch. There was a carton of milk on the table and a sandwich on a plate. "Do you want something to eat?" he asked. "I just made some bacon. I'm having a bacon and egg sandwich."

"No, thank you," said Laura. She could smell the bacon and her stomach lurched, but she tried to seem calm. It was amazing to see Billy when she'd been expecting Gabrielle. Nice, really. She was aware of his eyes upon her body.

"Where's your sister?" she asked. "I thought she didn't go to work until afternoon."

"Right, but she and my mother went over to Annie Sez shopping. Gabrielle just got her first paycheck."

"Oh," said Laura, and looked down at the table.

Billy ate some of his sandwich. "I was sorry to hear about your mother. A real tragedy."

Laura nodded, her eyes filling with tears. Sometimes when she hadn't been thinking about her mother and people were direct, it affected her like this. She was taken by surprise, and she felt real pain wash over her.

"It's okay," said Billy. "I'd cry, too."

Change the subject, Laura warned herself, *or else you'll really start crying.* She concentrated on Billy's face. He'd become a man since she'd last seen him, with bony features and a dark look to his jaw. His face was like his father's.

She suddenly remembered what Gabrielle had said. "Your sister said you're dealing cards now."

"That's right. Blackjack."

"What's it like in a casino? I always wondered. I used to go to some of those hotels in Atlantic City when I was little. Our parents would take us out to dinner or maybe to a floor show, but no one in our family ever gambled."

Billy walked over to the refrigerator. "Are you sure you don't want anything?" he asked. "Just say the word."

"Well, maybe some juice and toast if you have it. Actually I haven't eaten anything yet."

"I thought so," Billy said. He put an English muffin into the toaster oven and leaned on the counter, waiting.

"Aren't you going to tell me about the casino?" Laura persisted, sitting at the table. She discovered she really was interested in what he would say.

There was a silence. Even the music in the other room had stopped. "Casinos are weird places," said Billy. "You don't want to know about them."

"Yes I do."

"How old are you now? Are you Gabrielle's age?"

Laura nodded.

"People who gamble aren't having fun," said Billy. "That's the first thing you need to know."

"Why do they do it then?"

"Who knows? I guess there are different reasons." He poured some juice and brought Laura the English muffin.

"The other night a guy punched me in the face because he lost a hand. Does that sound like fun?"

"But it wasn't your fault, was it?"

"Of course not," said Billy, "but everyone blames the dealer." He looked at her plate. "You're not eating your breakfast."

Laura forced herself to have some of the English muffin. It was a relief to her that she could actually eat in front of Billy, someone she hardly knew. "How come you deal blackjack, instead of, say, poker?"

"They don't have poker in the casinos."

"What else *do* they have?"

Billy counted on his fingers. "Craps, roulette, the wheel of fortune. The slot machines, of course."

"Do certain people always play certain games?"

"They tend to," said Billy. "Hey, you really ask a lot of questions, don't you?" He smiled at her happily and leaned back in his chair.

Laura began to feel on familiar ground. She was a beautiful girl and she knew it. Her beauty was like an important family possession. "Isn't she lovely," her mother would say when introducing her to others. "My little girl is going to break a lot of hearts someday," said her father.

Laura had thick dark hair, a wide mouth, and high cheekbones. She'd developed early, menstruating at eleven, and her figure was full and round, like a movie star's from the fifties. She wasn't conceited. She didn't care about being beautiful, but it gave her a certain kind of freedom. It gave her confidence.

16

She said to Billy, "I want to come to the casino with you. Bring me sometime?"

Abruptly he went into the living room. Another tape began playing. This time it was piano music, something that sounded like jazz.

"I can't do that," he said when he came back. "You have to be twenty-one to get into the casinos. Besides, when I'm there, I'm working. I'm not even supposed to talk to anyone. There are all kinds of bosses looking over my shoulder. The pit boss, he's always within inches, and then the people who check up on him come by. There are even cameras in the ceiling taking pictures of the action at the tables."

The more Billy said, the more Laura wanted to go to the casinos. If there was that much security, whatever was going on there had to be pretty exciting, she thought. Not money changing hands, but some kind of edge of danger attracted her.

"But listen," Billy went on, "that doesn't mean we can't do something together. How about Sunday? I get off at six and my buddy has a boat moored over in the bay. He lets me use it sometimes. If the sky is clear, there'll be a great sunset. I'll pick you up at seven."

Just then they heard the sound of a car in the driveway. "It's my mother and Gabrielle," Billy said. "What about Sunday?"

"Sure," answered Laura. Suddenly there was a feeling of haste and secrecy to their plans. Billy didn't want his family to know about them for some reason. That was fine with

17

Laura. She went to the kitchen door. Gabrielle and her mother were taking their packages out of the trunk and she saw Mrs. Ruzzo squeeze Gabrielle's shoulder.

Laura's mother had always wanted to take her shopping at Annie Sez, too. It was an enormous store with designer clothing and everything marked down. Every August her mother and Heather would spend most of a day there, going out to lunch and buying Heather what she needed for school. But Laura wasn't interested. She liked to buy her clothes in Manhattan, at The Gap or in secondhand stores.

Laura went outside to greet Gabrielle and her mother. The wind had come up, blowing the sand near the driveway. She was a little chilly in her sundress. She took the packages Mrs. Ruzzo was carrying and kissed her on the cheek.

"Laura, Laura, let me get a look at you," Mrs. Ruzzo said. "Why did you wait until now to come?" Without another word she put her arms around Laura and folded her in.

It was Gabrielle's mother's unbearable kindness that had made her stay away from the Ruzzos, Laura suddenly realized, not the fight with Gabrielle at all. Pressed against Mrs. Ruzzo she felt strange and guilty, and she wasn't sure what she was expected to do. She smelled powder and the damp, rich odor of perspiration and swayed momentarily on her feet.

"Mom, you're holding her too tight," said Gabrielle, sounding annoyed.

"Am I?" Mrs. Ruzzo moved back. "I'm sorry, Laura. It's very emotional for me to see you. You understand . . ."

"Did you just get here?" Gabrielle asked. "Did you see my brother?"

Laura nodded, trying to keep her face neutral. A guilty excitement went through her.

"Isn't it wonderful that he's home?" said Mrs. Ruzzo. "I can't tell you how happy we are. . . . all those long trips in the merchant marine. I worried whenever the ocean was rough.

"Did Gabrielle tell you Marna's pregnant? Four months. . . . the baby's due in November. She'll be out Saturday for dinner. Why don't you come, too? I know she'd love to see you."

"My father and Heather will be here. But maybe I could come another time," Laura said. She trailed behind Mrs. Ruzzo and Gabrielle into the house. Billy had disappeared.

"Come to my room, Laura. I'll show you what I got." Gabrielle led the way upstairs to her bedroom and dropped her packages on the unmade bed. Gabrielle's room was always a mess.

She took out a pink and black dress with a black stretch waist, holding it up to herself and looking in the bureau mirror. "You want to see this on me?" she asked, stepping out of her skirt. "You're not still mad at me, are you?"

"I never was. But I'm sorry if I hurt your feelings. I didn't mean anything about Greg."

"I thought you might be jealous," Gabrielle said. "I mean, here I am with a boyfriend and living at home with my family. . . ."

"No, really, Gabrielle. I'm happy for you." Laura moved farther away, out of range of the mirror. "Sometimes my

19

reactions to things are strange, that's all. Since my mother died, it's made me kind of pessimistic."

"I know what you mean."

The two girls were silent for a moment, admiring Gabrielle's new dress. Then Gabrielle changed again, putting on a gray uniform with a notched white collar. *Food services*, read a patch over her heart. "I have to hurry or I'll be late to work. Want to walk me to the bus?"

"Why not?" said Laura.

Downstairs Mrs. Ruzzo was sitting at the dining room table reading the newspaper. "Hello, girls." She stood up and pushed Laura toward the kitchen. "Wait here," she told Gabrielle.

"Please sit, Laura. I'm worried about you." Obediently Laura sat down. No one ever argued with Mrs. Ruzzo. "You've lost your mother and that's a terrible thing. My own mother died when I was thirty-eight and I still felt like an orphan. At thirty-eight, can you imagine?

"Gabrielle told me about your swim in the ocean. You have to be more careful. . . . Promise me you will be."

Heat came into Laura's face. She nodded, not daring to speak.

"We've known you ever since you were small. Don't be such a stranger, anymore. . . . I want you to come visit me. Come anytime. I only work two days a week now."

"All right," Laura agreed. She could see Gabrielle waiting in the doorway with her back toward them.

They left the house and walked a block and a half to Pacific Avenue. Here, farther from the ocean, trees shaded the sidewalks and the air was still. As they came to the corner, they could see a bus coming. Gabrielle already had a dollar in her hand. "See you soon," she told Laura.

As the bus pulled away from the curb, Laura read its sign. The buses often advertised the casinos. AT HARRAH'S, EVERYBODY IS SOMEBODY, this one said. The picture showed two dice against a bright sunset.

Laura smiled to herself and walked slowly home.

CHAPTER
3

It was Friday night. Laura was in the backyard, watching the charcoal in the barbecue grill heat up. She'd decided to cook dinner for her father and Heather and a barbecue seemed easiest.

It had been hard for Laura, handling the raw hamburger meat, but she'd done it anyway. She wanted her father to see that she was better, so that he'd be proud of her and not worry.

Their backyard in Ventnor was surrounded by a high hedge. A gardener came once a week and clipped it and cut the lawn. He must have come today while she was sleeping, thought Laura, because the patio was littered with grass clippings. It was a humid, overcast evening. The leaves on the hydrangea bushes hardly moved.

Suddenly the screened porch door flew open with a crack. Her father had arrived. "Laura! Let me look at you," he said, grabbing her from behind.

Danny Samuels was a big man with a full head of stiff gray hair. He wore it in a crew cut and had it cut every two weeks. He was quite vain about his hair. Despite the heat he was wearing a business suit and vest, but his tie was loose at his throat. When he kissed Laura, she could smell the cigars he smoked.

Right behind him was Heather, with her overnight bag still in her hand. "How are you, Laura?" she asked, but did not wait for an answer. "I see you set the dining room table for three. But we have a guest. Well, kind of a guest anyway. . . ." She stopped talking and looked at Laura's bare feet. A tall man came onto the screened porch.

"Laura, this is Leo Kramer. Leo was one of my professors at law school last semester. I already told Daddy so I better tell you. . . . Leo and I are engaged. We're going to get married in September."

"Where?" asked Laura. It was a strange question to ask, but all the other questions would be unacceptable. Like *Why?* for example. *Why get married when your mother died last month? Why in September when you're supposed to be here with me this summer? Why this man, who must be at least forty and is thin as a rail and almost entirely bald?*

Heather squinted at Laura suspiciously, as if she were judging Laura's thoughts. She was wearing a pink linen suit, pink sandals, and a string of pearls that had belonged to their mother. Her style was like their mother's, too, cool and perfect.

23

"The wedding will be in New York. In our apartment. Where else?" She put her arm around Leo and moved him forward. "Aren't you going to congratulate us?"

"Congratulations," Laura said.

The Samuels girls. Their lives as sisters had never been smooth. When they were young, they had terrible physical fights which Heather always won, being bigger by far. Laura became a biter in self-defense, and once when she broke the skin on her sister's arm, her mother caught her and bit her back to teach her a lesson, but that only made things worse. As they grew older, their fighting became secretive, with threats and blackmail used as weapons. Since Laura tended to push the limits, Heather always had something to hold over her head. "If you don't give me five dollars, I'll tell Mommy you lied about where you were Friday night."

But they could be close, too. In May when their mother had died, Heather had let Laura come into her bed every night for a week and had stroked her hair and held her. Was she already seeing Leo then? She must have been.

Laura felt ill. She shuddered and turned away from Heather. "I'll go put the coleslaw and rolls and things on the table. It looks like the hamburgers are almost ready."

In the kitchen she dropped her head over the sink. Blood was pounding against her skull. Once or twice in her life, she'd had migraines, headaches so fierce they made her throw up. Laura hoped she was not going to get a migraine now.

At dinner everyone sat in their usual places. Heather had set a place for Leo, putting it on the side of the table nearest the kitchen door, where their mother had always sat. Laura also noticed that she'd switched the silverware and china, using the good white bone plates and sterling silver. Laura wondered how something like that could matter. Did Heather really think it would make Leo more impressed with them?

Yet he was actually commenting on the china, lifting up a plate to read the trademark underneath. "Ah, English. I thought so. Lovely."

"They belonged to my grandmother," Heather said. "More macaroni salad, Leo?"

"Yes, I think I will." He held out his plate.

Laura's headache was worse and now she felt nauseated, too. She closed her eyes and tried to swallow.

"Aren't you hungry?" Laura's father asked, using a piece of his hard roll to scoop up the liquid left from the coleslaw. "I thought you'd licked that problem. You told me on the phone you were eating again."

"I had a big lunch," said Laura. "Excuse me." She pushed her plate back and left the dining room, trying not to appear to hurry. Then, the moment she was out of sight, she put her hand over her mouth and raced for the bathroom.

But, though she stayed crouched on the floor in front of the toilet bowl, Laura could not vomit. At last she went into her bedroom. She drew the shades and got into bed with all her clothes on. She knew from experience that she'd have to wait out the headache, lying perfectly still in her bed until she relaxed enough to go to sleep.

The bedroom door opened, casting the hall light directly

25

onto her face. "What's the matter with you?" asked Heather from the doorway.

"I have a headache, a really bad one." Laura pulled up her knees and covered her eyes with her forearm. "I'm sorry I had to leave."

"Well, I guess it's okay then. We thought you were up here sulking."

Laura groaned. "Good night," she said and turned away from her sister. The door clicked shut.

She lay awake for a long time. The dining room was directly underneath her bed and she could hear the hum of conversation. It reminded her of being a little girl put to bed when her parents had dinner parties. Now she was still upstairs while Heather acted like her mother, asking everyone if they wanted any more and passing around the vegetables. But surely Heather couldn't think that marrying someone like Leo would give her a place in the world.

Laura could feel anger at her sister burn through her. "Forget it," she cautioned herself, "or you're never going to get to sleep." She concentrated only on her breath, going in and out of her lungs, and then, finally, she did sleep.

The next morning it was raining. Great sheets of rain washed over the house and the wind was blowing hard. When Laura awoke, the air was so dark and tumultuous she felt as if she were on a ship at sea. The alarm clock told her it was after twelve o'clock. Her body was sore but as she turned her head from side to side, she discovered with gratitude that her headache was gone.

She went downstairs and found her father at the kitchen

26

table playing solitaire. The overhead light shone down on the white formica surface, making it like an island. Heather and Leo were nowhere in sight.

"Where are the lovebirds?" Laura asked, putting the kettle on for coffee.

"Don't be sarcastic. They went to Brigantine, shopping for furniture for Leo's apartment. You should be happy for your sister."

"Why?" asked Laura.

"Leo's a nice man. He's reliable. Heather made a good choice."

"I don't agree. And what's she doing getting married when her mother just died?"

"I don't see what that has to do with it. She's twenty-two years old. She can get married when she wants to." Laura's father dealt himself several more cards.

The kettle boiled, letting out a piercing whine. Laura took it off the stove and made a cup of instant coffee. She said to her father, "Do you know how to play blackjack?"

"Of course."

"Can you teach me how to play it?"

Laura's father put his palms on the edge of the table and looked at her directly. "What's this? You never showed an interest in cards before."

"So?" Laura shrugged. "Everything changes. Heather's getting married. I want to learn to play cards. What's so strange about that?"

Her father shuffled the cards and cut them. "Sit down," he told Laura.

"The object of the game is to come as close to twenty-one as you can, but not go over it. Face cards are worth ten, aces are either one or eleven."

"You mean kings and queens are face cards?" Laura asked.

"Right. And jacks. For instance . . ." He dealt them each two cards, one down and one showing. "Look at your cards, but don't show me the bottom one," he said. "How do they seem?"

"Good, I think," said Laura. Her top card was a nine and her bottom card was a queen. Nineteen points.

"Okay, now you have a choice. You can either bet on what you have, assuming your cards are closer to twenty-one than mine are. Or you can bet and ask for another card."

Laura studied the stylized face of her queen as if it would give her an answer. "What if I don't want to bet?"

"If more people were playing or if there was a dealer, that would be all right. You could pass. But since it's just you and me, we both have to bet or there's no game. Tell you what . . ."

Her father went over to the cupboard and brought back a can of mixed nuts. He rubbed his hands together like a conjurer. "Hand me the can opener."

Laura got it from the drawer, amazed. She couldn't believe that her restless father was actually sitting and arranging mixed nuts on the kitchen table. "These are like chips. Like you bet with. Peanuts are pennies, walnuts are nickels, almonds are dimes, filberts are quarters."

"I'll bet four filberts."

"No, you have to say it in money."

"Okay," said Laura. "A dollar."

"You're pretty sure of your hand then?" He winked at her and grinned. "I'm going to see that bet and raise you a dollar." He counted out eight filberts and pushed them toward the center of the table. "Let's see your cards," he said.

Laura showed him. She was so fascinated by the ritual of counting and betting, she'd forgotten the point of the game. So when her father put down a jack and an ace and took all the filberts, she just stared at him.

"Twenty-one. I got twenty-one. Remember I said aces could be either one or eleven? Ten plus eleven is twenty-one." He shuffled the cards again. "Let's play a few more hands. What do you say?"

"Sure." It felt like the first time in almost a year that Laura's father had asked anything of her, the first time she'd had his full attention at all. Even when she'd been seeing Joseph, who had long hair and wore an earring, her father hadn't seemed to notice. But that was last winter, in March.

"You'd better make yourself some breakfast while you're at it," he said.

They played for almost two hours, hand after hand, while the rain drummed steadily outside. They didn't talk much, just placed their bets. At one point Laura's father asked if she wanted him to teach her poker or gin, but she declined.

"What's this fascination you have with blackjack?" he said.

"It's what they play in the casinos." She waited to see the effect of her words.

"The casinos! What do you know about the casinos?"

"Nothing. Just that they have blackjack there." She looked at him calmly. "I know I'm too young to go to a casino."

"Damn right you are." Laura's father put down his cards and ran his hand over his face.

Suddenly a door opened and the fluorescent light went on, erasing the shadows at the edges of the room. Heather and Leo had come back. Laura and her father glanced at each other in an almost guilty way. The intimacy that had been between them was gone.

Heather said, "Why was it so dark in here? How can you even see?"

"Did you buy anything?" asked Laura's father. He loved people to spend money, the more the better, though in fact he had no interest in what they actually purchased with it.

"We saw some nice carpeting, in just the color we need. But we want to price it in New York before making up our minds," said Leo. He smiled at Laura. "Are you feeling better? Heather said you had quite a headache last night."

"Much better. All better, in fact," said Laura.

Leo wasn't as ugly as she'd thought at first. There was something comical and delicate about his face that partly made up for his high bald forehead. He had smooth, fine skin and light brown eyes that held her gaze.

"What're these cards doing on the table?" Heather picked up the deck and moved it to the top of the refrigerator. "I'm starved. We didn't get any lunch."

She took out the plastic containers of deli leftovers. "Isn't there anything else beside this stuff?"

"It looks fine to me," Leo said. "Were you two playing cards?"

Laura's father lit a cigar. "Not in here while I'm eating, please," said Heather.

He opened the window over the kitchen sink and stood before it, turning the cigar between his fingers. "I was teaching Laura blackjack," he said. "She seems to have inherited my interest in cards."

"Well, you're living in the right place then," Leo said. "Do you ever get to the casinos?"

"My wife and I used to go when they first opened, but we haven't gone in years." Laura noticed the way his sentence sounded as if they might still change their minds at any time. Through the open window, a fine spray of rain blew in, scenting the air with freshness.

"Billy Ruzzo's a blackjack dealer at Trump Plaza." Laura had been wanting to say Billy's name, but no one reacted.

"Do you play cards, Leo?" asked Laura's father.

"A little poker once a month with some other guys on the faculty. But it's not much. Low stakes."

"I have a great idea," said Heather. She glanced at Laura. "Let's go to the casinos tonight. We can get all dressed up and spend some money. We'll each have a limit of what we can lose. Twenty-five dollars, say, or fifty."

"What about me? What am I supposed to do?" Laura asked. *Please, tell her to forget it*, she pleaded mentally with her father. *Don't leave me here alone again.*

"Would you like to have dinner in Margate, at the Sailfish Café?" He came over and put his arm around Laura. "Then

31

we'll drop you at home and go in to Atlantic City. You won't mind that. We'll only stay an hour or two."

Leo spoke up then. "It doesn't seem quite fair to Laura, to do something she can't do—"

"Laura will understand," her father said confidently. "It'll be a good way for me to get to know you, Leo. To see what kind of husband you'll be for Heather. You can tell a lot about a man by the way he plays cards."

"That's ridiculous," said Laura. "What do cards and love have in common?"

"More than you might think," her father said. And even Leo nodded.

CHAPTER
4

At midnight the rain stopped. Laura took a mohair stole of her mother's and walked barefoot onto the beach. The sand felt soft and cool between her toes, and foghorns at sea called gently to each other. It was a misty night without any moon. At first Laura only looked out at the vast darkness of the water. But on her way back, she saw the lights of Atlantic City rising in tiers, pale and dewy, magnified by the mist.

Right here, just a mile or two away, a new world was waiting. It had been here all along and yet she'd never really thought of it before. Laura imagined crowds of elegantly dressed people, moving through spacious rooms with cocktails in their hands. Soon she would be among them.

At dinner she'd persuaded her father to let her stay in the

house another week. "All spring when Mommy was sick, the only thing I could think about was coming to Ventnor," she'd said. "Why should I suffer just because Heather won't be here?"

The three of them didn't return from Atlantic City until two. She heard the cab stop at the curb, then Leo's voice and her father's booming laugh outside. Laura ran downstairs to greet them.

Everyone's clothes smelled of cigarette smoke, and Heather's cheeks were flushed. "How was it?" Laura asked.

"Weird. Weird, weird, weird," said Heather.

"What do you mean?"

"A bunch of lost souls," Laura's father said. "Go to bed. We'll tell you about it tomorrow."

But they never did. The next morning before Laura even woke up, the others had decided to play golf.

"How can I play? I don't know how," complained Laura. She was in Heather's room, watching her sister get dressed.

"But it's so pretty at the club. Just follow along with us. Come for the ride. We're all going."

"Daddy, too? Are you sure?"

Heather nodded. That settled it because Laura wanted to spend more time with her father. They were all leaving at five to go back to the city.

She sat down on Heather's bed. Leo had slept in the guest room. "When did you learn to play golf?"

"In the spring," said Heather. "Leo's a fanatic." Their parents had been fanatics, too. On weekends, when her father came down to Ventnor, they usually played both

34

days. Their mother had won second place in a tournament for women forty and over last summer. *Last summer.*

Heather stood in front of the mirror, brushing her hair. Laura had always envied Heather's hair. It was red, almost copper, with deep waves in it. "I wanted Daddy to play. I thought it would do him good. He can't keep avoiding all the places he used to go with Mommy."

But this morning Laura's father was in an expansive mood. He took them out for breakfast, then ordered a limousine to drive them to the golf course. He even insisted they get a golf cart. "You drive, Laura," he said, perhaps trying to make up for leaving her home the night before.

At her parents' country club in Somer's Point, the air was blue and sparkling, washed clean from the rain. Laura steered the golf cart from one hole to another and sat under the white canvas awning as Heather and Leo and her father set up their shots and took them. They were enjoying themselves but she couldn't tell why. The green was crowded and there were people waiting in line at every hole.

"Don't you want to try this?" Leo asked her when they were at a sand trap. He handed her a club and stood behind her, showing her how to swing her arms with her elbows bent for the follow-through. "Try it. Hit it."

To Laura's surprise the ball spun out of the sand trap and landed only a foot from the hole. Her father slapped Leo on the back. "What do you think of that?" he said. "Both my girls are natural athletes."

Nine holes were enough, they decided. More than enough, Laura thought privately. What a stupid game! And what if you were hit by a golf ball? They were flying in all directions, small hard objects whizzing through the air at high speed. Surely one landing in just the right spot on the skull would kill you in an instant. "How many people die on golf courses?" she asked on their way back to the clubhouse.

"What? What do you mean?" her father said sharply. It had been an unspoken rule since her mother had gotten sick that nobody could mention death in any form. Even simple phrases like "I thought I was going to die" were to be avoided.

"Don't you think a golf ball could kill you?" Laura persisted anyway.

"That's stupid," Heather said. "I'm sure more old men die of heart attacks on golf courses than ever die of golf balls."

The Somer's Point clubhouse was a sprawling white building with a dining room and deck overlooking Great Bay. Gaily colored sailboats dotted the water and in the sky overhead a small plane pulled a banner saying DISCOVER SHOWBOAT, ATLANTIC CITY'S NEWEST CASINO HOTEL.

Everyone ordered lunch but Laura wanted only club soda and fruit salad. Heather and Leo had gone to call some friends in the city and across the table from her, her father was reading the real estate section of the Sunday *Times*. The dining room was full and busy. Nobody was paying any attention to Laura.

She reached down under the fold of the tablecloth. Just as she'd hoped, Heather had left her purse on her chair. It was a leather purse with a simple clasp. Laura undid it and, keeping her eyes on her father, she felt around until her hand closed over Heather's wallet. Quickly she transferred it to her own pocketbook. Then she hung her sister's purse over the back of the chair, leaving the clasp open.

Heather and Leo came back to the table. Their shrimp cocktails had arrived, displayed on beds of chopped ice. "Mmmm, that looks delicious," said Leo. But Laura couldn't bear to see the tiny creatures, each one so curved and pink. She asked for a section of the newspaper and held it in front of her face.

It was after dessert that Heather discovered her wallet was gone. She and Leo had insisted on paying the check. "I can't believe this," she said, looking under the table, then standing up and putting her hands in her pockets. This isn't possible."

"What isn't? What's the matter, Heather?" asked Leo.

"My wallet's been stolen. I left it right here in my purse."

"Waiter!" said Laura's father. He stood up and beckoned, using his whole arm to call the boy who'd served them back to their table. "Did you see this woman's wallet?"

"No, sir."

"Are you sure?" Laura's father demanded. "Would you like me to call the manager?"

The boy was younger than Laura, probably only fifteen or sixteen. He had bad skin and oily black hair that lay flat on his forehead. Laura felt sorry for him, but there was nothing she could do. She needed Heather's I.D., her driver's license that said she was twenty-two.

The boy was brave, though. "Call him if you want," he said. "I didn't take her wallet."

Heather put her hand on her father's arm. "Dad, please. It could be anyone. Look at this place. It's packed. Leo will pay the bill. Let's just get out of here."

"Goddamn it, Heather. Don't tell me what to do!" He shook Heather's hand free.

It wasn't the first time their father had made a scene in a restaurant. Either the soup was cold or the roast beef was too well done or the service was bad. He figured that as the customer he had a right to object. But Laura's mother could always calm him down. She'd get him laughing or touch his arm and whisper something to him and he'd relax.

Laura and Heather looked at each other and Laura knew they were thinking the same thing. She was amazed that they could be here at all, the four of them, on a bright June day, eating and talking as if her mother did not exist. Because really she was in everything they did and said. She was with them every minute.

Laura clutched her pocketbook with Heather's wallet inside and got up from the table. *Move slowly*, she commanded herself, *don't rush*. Maybe if she began to leave, her father would follow. Sometimes with her father, the best course was just to give him a way out. Good, it was working. He and Heather were both coming. Only Leo stayed behind, paying the bill and talking to the waiter.

As they waited for the limousine to pick them up, Laura went into the bathroom. She locked the metal stall door and looked through Heather's wallet. Her New York driver's license had Heather's picture on it. Laura thought they looked nothing alike, but people who didn't know them well always commented on the resemblance. In the picture Heather was wearing a black beret that hid her hair. The guards at the casinos would never be able to tell she wasn't Heather.

The limousine had come. It was parked outside in the curved gravel driveway. Everyone had already taken their places. "I gave the manager your number in Ventnor, Laura," said Leo to her quietly.

The driver had an all-news station on the radio and Laura's father and Heather were leaning forward, listening to it. "He'll call the police about Heather's wallet and if they find it, they'll get in touch with you," Leo said.

Laura's mouth went dry. Would they want to prosecute her for stealing her sister's wallet? But the wallet was never mentioned again. By the time they got back to Ventnor, everyone had to pack so they could catch the five-thirty helicopter back to New York. "Are you sure you don't want to come? I could probably make another reservation," said her father, standing next to his bag in the hallway.

"No, thanks. It'll probably be a hundred and ten degrees in the city. I'd rather stay here."

"But what'll you do all week?"

"She'll be fine," said Heather. "How are the Ruzzos, Laura? Didn't you mention that Billy was home? Is he still as handsome as he used to be?"

"I don't think he's handsome," Laura said. But of course it was a lie. She pictured Billy's bony face. It filled her thoughts after the others had left, and for a while it even filled the echoing rooms.

The door to her mother's dressing room was closed, but Laura pushed it open and turned on the light. She was wearing a blue silk shirt and white silk pants that she'd found in Heather's closet. Immediately her reflection surrounded her. There were mirrors on every wall and mirrored doors in the closets. When she was young, Laura had loved the way her reflection went on and on in this room, repeating into infinity.

She sat down at her mother's dressing table. Cut glass perfume bottles were arranged in a row across the back and there were lacquered trays of makeup, a different tray for every kind—eye shadow, eyebrow pencils and mascaras, lipsticks, foundation and powder, blushers and rouge.

The strange thing, thought Laura, was that her mother never seemed really made-up. Her face was always smooth and perfect, though, with rosy lips and cheekbones, and smudged, smoky eyelids. She looked ageless. That was how Laura wanted to look, too. Billy would see a different girl when he came to pick her up tonight, a girl who could easily be a twenty-two-year-old woman.

All through her teens, Laura had never worn makeup. In this way she was different from her mother and her sister and from every other girl at school with her in Manhattan. That's why she'd done it in the first place.

"Don't you care how you look?" her mother had pleaded, trying to interest her in a beauty parlor haircut or new clothes or a makeup special offered by one of the big department stores. "But this is how I look," answered Laura every time. She knew she was beautiful enough to get by.

But not to get into the casinos. She wiped her face with a tissue and dotted foundation on it, the way she'd seen her mother do. Her eyes and nostrils immediately became stronger—dark round shapes popping out at her. Laura chose green eye shadow for her eyes, which were also green, and put pink blusher across her cheeks.

She looked very odd to herself, pale and masklike, but when she tried to use her mother's mascara, it was a disaster. The top of the tube hadn't been put on right and the mascara was half-solid, clumping in lumps on her eyelashes. Laura tried to rub it off with some cotton, but it only smeared more and got into her eyes. They watered and stung painfully. She felt as if she were going blind.

She groped her way into her parents' bathroom and splashed cold water across her face. When she finally opened her eyes again, she looked like a raccoon with the mascara in black circles on her face.

Just at that moment, the doorbell rang. It was Billy, who had come to pick her up. He was twenty minutes early, Laura saw on her watch, but it didn't matter. There was no way she could go downstairs now.

The bell rang and rang, but she did not answer it. Instead she drew the curtain in the bathroom window and sat on the toilet, hot and miserable, until he went away. At exactly seven she called the Ruzzos, praying that Mr. or Mrs. Ruzzo would not answer. She was in luck. "Hello?" said Billy's voice after only the first ring.

"Billy? I'm really sorry." Laura improvised. "It turned out that I had to do something for my father tonight. He wanted me to pick something up for him and send it first

41

thing tomorrow. Can we go out in the boat another time? Later on in the week maybe? I really want to do that."

"It's okay. Don't worry about it."

"But can we go another time?"

"Sure," said Billy. There was a silence.

"Are you mad at me?"

"No, it's just . . . I was looking forward to it. I made all the arrangements to get the boat and everything."

"How about tomorrow night? Could we go then?"

"I guess so," said Billy. "But listen, if you don't want to go out with me, just say so."

"No, I do. Really." Suddenly Laura felt desperate to make him believe her. "When I see you tomorrow night, I'll prove it," she said.

"You will, huh?" Billy's voice changed, becoming both softer and deeper. "Is seven o'clock still good?"

"I'll be ready," said Laura.

CHAPTER
5

Laura looked at her alarm clock in disbelief. It was six-thirty in the morning. This was the earliest she'd woken up in months and she had no idea how she was going to make the time pass. So many hours! She sat on the edge of her bed getting her bearings, then she walked over to the window. A thick fog covered Marion Avenue like a wall. The sun wouldn't burn it off until noon, if then.

But when she went into the kitchen and turned on the radio, there was a broadcast announcing the acts that were playing in the casinos. The really famous comedians and singers only performed at night, of course, but in all the bars and hotel lounges, groups with names like "The Policeman's Ball" and "Rocket and the Blasters" would be entertaining patrons every hour on the hour.

Billy worked days, too, thought Laura. She was supposed to see him tonight anyway. Why not go to Trump Plaza and find him right now? Her spirits lifted. She made herself some toast and thought about how she would do it.

She knew where Trump's was. In Atlantic City all the casino hotels were right on the boardwalk, facing the sea. Behind them was the city itself, a ghetto with pawnshops and pornographic bookstores and young black men prowling the streets. When people had to drive through Atlantic City, they always locked the car doors.

But Laura was used to New York. She'd been in much worse neighborhoods plenty of times. She liked the Lower East Side for its weird mixture of punk kids, old Polish and Jewish people, and junkies. When she'd been just a freshman, she and her friends would go down on Sunday afternoons when the street vendors displayed their wares on tablecloths on the sidewalks. Her parents never knew about it. She'd tell them she was going to a museum.

Laura considered what to wear to the casino. She wanted to look sophisticated, worldly. Not like a high school girl. She pictured a dress with a low-cut neckline and pleats that swirled when she moved. Her mother's closet was the place to look for such a dress, Laura knew, but upstairs she kept hesitating, unable for some reason to open the closet doors.

When at last she did and saw every dress and blouse and pair of shoes her mother ever wore in summertime, Laura was overcome with the strongest memory she'd yet had of her mother. She could smell the perfume her mother wore and hear her voice, thin and insubstantial, ruffling through the room like a breeze. "Why are you doing this, Laura? You shouldn't be in here."

Laura jumped back from the edge of the closet. She was shivering and her skin felt damp. It was so much like something her mother would say. A sentence or two, just enough to make her feel guilty. *Stop it!* she told herself. She picked up the first pair of shoes she saw, a pair of black patent leather pumps, but could not bring herself to take anything else.

She'd wear her black sundress and maybe she'd buy a new dress in Atlantic City. Her father had given Laura and Heather Visa and American Express cards the week after their mother died. "I'll pay the bills each month, if you promise to buy the things you need and not bother me about it," he'd said.

Laura left the house, locking the door behind her. Her mother's pumps hurt when she walked. It had been years since she'd worn high heels. Probably the last time was when she was twelve or thirteen and all her Philadelphia cousins were getting bar mitzvahed. That was the last time she'd allowed her mother to tell her what to wear, too.

At the bus stop, a small knot of people stood waiting. A few had on uniforms. There was a waitress, and two men in maroon suits were joking about another man who worked on their shift. Laura thought they might be porters or elevator operators.

At each stop more people crowded onto the bus. One fat black woman with a gray uniform straining at the seams offered a bag of sour balls around. "I take them for my cough," she said. "Help yourselves. Feel free."

"Thanks," said Laura.

"Not before my morning coffee," said the waitress.

Laura was so absorbed in her fantasies about the bus riders and their jobs that she stayed on the bus longer than she meant to. "Last stop. The Inlet." The driver looked back at her. "You don't want to get off here. Where you going, girl?"

"Oh, I'm sorry. To Trump Plaza. Did I miss my stop?"

"You just stay put. I'll tell you when." He swung the wheel around and started on his return journey. At this end of the route all the people who got on the bus were black. The driver was black, too.

"This is it. Trump's. You got to walk down a block, over to Atlantic."

"Thanks a lot," said Laura. She stepped down and was left standing alone on a corner, in a world that seemed gray and abandoned. But as she turned she could see the gleaming bulk of a casino rising above tenements and storefronts. She clutched her pocketbook and walked toward it.

Arriving in the lobby, Laura discovered that blisters were already forming on her heels. There was a shop that sold newspapers and small toiletries and she asked the girl behind the cash register about stockings. "Taupe or nude?" the girl asked, and Laura said, "Nude." But she forgot to ask where a bathroom was.

The lobby was a huge vaulted place with marble pillars and pendulous crystal chandeliers. Everything was polished. Everything sparkled. There were mirrors on some of the walls, making it hard to tell just where you were or even what was real. Laura could see herself reflected on several surfaces. She looked so young! Her dress didn't hang right, it was longer in back, but the mirrors were tinted a rose color that added red highlights to her hair.

Guests were standing at the courtesy desk with their luggage next to them, people dressed in evening clothes were waiting near a bank of elevators, employees stood around idly, their functions unclear. "Excuse me," said Laura, walking up to a woman wearing a uniform with gold braid and a high stand-up collar. "Could you tell me where the casino is?"

For a long time the woman didn't say anything at all. Laura felt uneasy. She brought her feet together and stared down at her mother's black patent leather pumps, waiting.

"Go up the escalator to the mezzanine and you'll see it in front of you. But you're not going to be able to get in."

"What do you mean?" asked Laura. She had Heather's I.D. with her, but she didn't want to show it to anyone unless they asked.

"Casino's closed until ten. From four to ten." She took out a gold pocket watch. "It's eight-forty now."

"Oh. I thought they were open twenty-four hours."

"Not this one. Not any of them. Got to give the gamblers a rest."

"Thanks," said Laura, starting to walk away.

"Wait a minute," the woman said. Laura stopped. "How old are you?"

"Seventeen. I'm here with my parents. I was looking for them. They were playing blackjack when I went to sleep last night. They said they'd be back any minute."

"Oh, I see." The woman's voice was different now, more

47

sympathetic. "They might be in the coffee shop. The one on the seventh floor? Or you could look for them outside on the boardwalk."

"I think I'll do that. Thanks very much." Laura moved toward the exit, aware that she was wobbling a little in the high heels. But probably it only added to the effect of her vulnerability. She wondered how many children were abandoned in Atlantic City because of their parents' gambling.

She had almost two hours to kill before she could find Billy. And it wasn't a good sign that the first hotel employee she'd talked to had asked her about her age. Laura walked along the boardwalk, thinking it over. When she'd gone only a block, she came to the next casino. This was Caesar's, a white and orange building with huge Roman plaster of paris statues set in niches next to the entrance. Laura went in.

The lobby was startlingly like the one at Trump's except that the ceilings were lower. Across from the elevators was a directory of restaurants and services provided to guests and visitors to the hotel. There was a beauty parlor on the third floor. Laura took the elevator up.

OPEN 24 HOURS, said a sign outside. CUTS, PERMANENTS, HAIR COLORING. FREE MANICURE OR MAKEUP WITH EVERY HAIRCUT.

Laura gave her name to a blonde woman at the counter. "Are you staying at this hotel?" she asked Laura.

"Yes."

"Your room number?"

"Nine fourteen," said Laura, her stomach seeming to fall out from under her with the lie.

48

But the woman simply wrote it down. Like the password to a secret kingdom, the number had gotten her in. Laura felt really excited and curious. Anything was possible. She might be someone else, a stranger, when she left.

"Ready?" A young man wearing blue jeans and a silk shirt led her to a big upholstered chair and placed a pink smock around her neck. "I'm Jason," he said. "And what would we like today?"

Both of them gazed at Laura in the mirror. "I want a more sophisticated look, but I'm not sure what."

Jason nodded. "Something close to the head, to bring out the cheekbones. But a shampoo first, yes?"

Laura stopped thinking. The sensations she felt were so pleasurable that she gave herself up to them entirely. Hot water, fingers massaging cool, sweet-smelling liquids through her hair, hands holding her hair, scissors cutting it, waves of heat and wind coming at her. "Voilà," said the hairdresser, Jason. "You must open your eyes now."

She was amazed to see herself. Her hair, which had been inches below her shoulders with ragged bangs, had become a sleek, shining cap. When she moved her head, it swung heavily with its own weight, like a curtain.

"I love it!" exclaimed Laura.

"Yes, it's very nice, I think." He started to take off the smock.

"But what about makeup?" Laura asked. "I thought it was included."

"Just a moment." Jason went into the front of the shop and returned with the receptionist. "She will do it," he said and walked away.

"Do you know how?" Laura asked the woman, alarmed.

"Certainly. I was only sitting out there because our regular receptionist isn't here yet. It's only nine-thirty, you know. The women don't usually start coming until the casino opens. They like to come here when their husbands are gambling." She placed her fingers gently on Laura's cheeks, then she led her to a small table where colors and brushes were laid out.

So many layers were necessary. Not just foundation, but a layer of cream, a moisturizer, the woman explained. Then a violet tint, to remove a slight sallowness, she explained. She was like Laura's dentist in Manhattan, appearing to believe that if Laura were told everything, she'd feel better.

"Don't make me look too natural," Laura said.

"But you've got a beautiful face. Why should we change it?"

"I look too young."

"Do you know how old the models in *Vogue* magazine are?" asked the woman, moving closer to Laura's face, working on her eyes now.

"In their twenties? Twenty-four or -five?"

"They're younger than you are," the woman said triumphantly. She used a lip pencil and some gloss on Laura's mouth, and then she said, "Close your eyes," and sprayed Laura's face with an atomizer. "I think you're done. You can look now."

Every feature seemed more colorful and definite, yet every mark on her skin had vanished. In a strange way Laura looked anonymous, not like herself, but anyone. She didn't mind this at all. It was even what she'd been looking for.

"Would you like to buy some of the products I used on your face?" the makeup artist asked.

"What time is it?"

"It's after ten. We could just add them to your bill."

"Fine," said Laura. "Do that."

Carrying a miniature paper shopping bag, she went down the elevator, back to Trump's and into the casino at last. There were guards at the entrance, but this time no one stopped her.

It was a vast red room, she could hardly see to the end of it. A low jingle filled the air, of countless coins being fed into slot machines, of bells ringing as jackpots were struck, of chips being gathered by dealers, of money changing hands. On her right was a row of cages like a bank, with tellers waiting to change money or redeem customers' chips. This felt like Laura's first major move as Heather Samuels, twenty-two years old since last October.

She went to the second window. "I'd like twenty dollars in quarters," she said, holding out a bill.

The teller was a woman in her thirties. She looked at Laura and seemed to hesitate. Then she handed her two rolls of quarters. "Good luck," she said.

Laura had decided to start with the slot machines. She knew Billy was out on the floor, in the middle of the casino, but she did not have the courage to find him yet. First, she thought, she'd try to win some money.

She stood behind a couple who were playing one of the dollar machines, silently taking turns pulling the handle down. They were middle-aged and overweight, and both wore glasses.

51

"How are you doing?" asked Laura. This was totally unlike her, to just question strangers, but her haircut and the new way her face looked had changed her.

The woman turned around. "Why, hi there, honey," she said with a Southern accent. "Last night we won eighty dollars off this machine, but now it's stealin' us blind. You want to take a turn? We're about done." She slung her purse over her shoulder and walked away.

"Good luck now," said her husband, following her down the aisle which was formed from slot machines lined on either side.

Laura opened her rolls of quarters and dumped them into her pocket. The machine took four quarters at a time. She inserted them into the slot and pulled the handle down. All her attention was concentrated on the little window and the spinning shapes, of oranges and grapefruits and grapes and apples. An apple and two lemons settled in a line.

She pulled the handle again and again until she had only a few quarters left in her pocket. By now Laura knew she would not walk away from this machine until all her money was gone. A few times some quarters came back to her and she fed them back into the slot again. Among the fruits there were dollar signs that were especially valuable. Laura pulled the handle, praying, actually praying, to win. Bells rang and lights flashed as three dollar signs settled in a line.

The machine seemed to vibrate with her victory. Other slot machine players came over to see what had happened. "That's twelve hundred-to-one odds, red dollar signs, three in a row like that!" an old black man exclaimed.

But meanwhile no quarters rang into the bowl at the bottom of the machine. "I don't understand," said Laura. "Where's the money?"

"They're going to have to verify it. You stay right here. Don't you leave this machine!" the black man said.

Laura turned around. There must have been a dozen people near her. They were plain people, dressed in regular clothes, like housewives or store clerks on their days off. Most of them looked tired, and they didn't really seem to be having a very good time.

"I don't believe it! What did I tell you, Fran. I said, 'Just watch, soon's we leave that machine, she's sure to hit it.' " It was the husband of the Southern couple talking. The two of them had moved next to Laura. They were crowding her on either side.

A heavy man dressed in a black pinstripe suit and carrying a notebook appeared then, "Who was playing this machine?" he asked in a self-important way.

"That woman there. She was," said the old black man.

"I was," Laura said. What was going to happen now? She was so lucky she had Heather's license. This morning she'd put Heather's charge cards in her wallet, too, just in case they asked to see something else.

"You've won quite a bit of money, Miss. Would you mind giving us some information?"

Laura shook her head.

"Name?"

"Heather Samuels.

"Date of birth?"

53

"October 11, 1966."

"Do you have any identification you could show us? Anything with your age on it?"

Laura gave him the driver's license and Heather's Visa card. The man in the black suit looked both documents over, his eyes moving from the picture to Laura's face. "Fine," he said. "Come with me, please."

The crowd moved back, muttering questions. "How much did she win? What do you want her to prove? Are you going to pay her or not?" But the man did not answer.

They went to the tellers' cages and he finished filling out a form in his notebook and pushed it across the counter. "How ya doin', Lou?" he greeted the teller.

"Slow morning so far. Can't complain." The teller counted out several new bills.

"Sorry to have held you up, Miss." The man in the black suit handed the money to Laura. "Good luck," were his last words to her.

Now that it was over, now that she'd gotten away with it, Laura did a little dance, swinging her arms and rocking her hips from side to side. The money was in her hands. Her own money, the first money she'd ever really made herself. She counted it, there by the tellers' cages. Twelve hundreds. $1200.00.

Laura could almost feel the adrenaline coursing through her body. She felt completely wired, ecstatically happy. "Could you tell me the time, please?" she asked a woman passing by.

"Why, yes. It's five to eleven."

She'd been standing before the slot machine for less than

an hour. It didn't seem possible. Time had vanished. Her family had vanished. She'd even forgotten about Billy. All her life seemed fixed at this point, like a crossroads between the past and the future.

She walked up to the teller's cage and said, "Could I change this for twenties? I want to play blackjack."

CHAPTER
6

The blackjack tables were the curved ones. They each had seven stools and the dealers stood inside the curves. Both men and women worked as dealers. Laura was surprised at that; she hadn't expected women. The dealers were black and white, Hispanic and Asian, and they all moved their hands continuously—laying out cards and chips, collecting cards and chips, never seeming to count or calculate, never even hesitating.

She wove between the lines of tables, trying to spot Billy. But when she finally did, Laura did not move closer. She was embarrassed suddenly, unwilling to be seen by him in her new haircut, her makeup. She knew she looked different, but she wasn't sure if she looked better or worse.

Billy was in a special roped-off section of the casino for baccarat, but there were also half-a-dozen blackjack tables with signs saying $50 MINIMUM BET. She thought this must be where the wealthy people gambled. Billy was standing like the other dealers, with his hands flying and his legs spread wide, fixed on what he was doing. Like the others, he was wearing black pants, a white shirt, and a vest shot through with metallic thread.

Only one player was at Billy's table, sitting on the far left stool. Instead of playing one hand, he played three at a time. As Laura watched, other players drifted in, played a few hands and went away. But the man to the left stayed on. He must be winning, Laura thought, because there was a big pile of chips in front of him. He fingered them as Billy was dealing, running his fingers along the sides of the little towers of chips, then letting the chips fall one by one to the table.

The game stopped. Billy gathered up the cards, and made two piles. There were so many cards, at least five or six decks. He shuffled them, about half a deck at a time, and put them into a long plastic box. A woman dressed in a black suit came over and stood next to Billy and took notes. Two more players drifted off. The man on the left stayed. Billy gave him a yellow card and he put it into the plastic box among the playing cards. The game began again.

What was going on? Laura felt as if she was watching an elaborate pantomime. No one said a word; gestures were everything. The atmosphere was charged, silent and intense, and the danger Laura had first imagined when Billy told her about the casinos was here after all. She looked into his face for reassurance and just then he glanced up and saw her, too.

She stepped closer and he dealt the gambler another three cards. Perhaps he hadn't recognized her. Laura came over to the table and stood directly behind the man who was playing. The gambler turned and smiled at her, but Billy's face was implacable, set and angry. When Laura saw the anger, she realized that though he knew she was there, he was not going to speak to her or react at all.

Screw him, thought Laura. *I can stay here if I want to; I've done nothing wrong.* At moments like this, when for example she had lied to her parents and been caught, Laura always felt like a wounded victim. She believed her own stories. And so in the casino she got angry at Billy. He should have known she was going to come; she'd said she wanted to.

"Would you like to sit down?" the gambler asked, indicating the stool next to him.

Billy's hands paused. "We try to save the seats for people who are playing."

"Fine," said the gambler. "When more people come, she'll move."

Laura sat down, self-conscious at interrupting the game. She couldn't tell what fascinated her more—the pattern of the cards and the chips piling up, or the face of the gambler, or Billy's hands dealing. The game she had played with her father at the kitchen table left her mind. This was different, so fast and complex that it seemed more like sleight of hand than a card game. She'd have to watch for a long time before she knew what to do.

The gambler won hand after hand. Laura tried to count his chips, but she kept losing track. The purple chips were five hundred dollars and she counted at least twenty or twenty-five of those, as well as lots of black hundred-dollar chips. He could have as much as twenty thousand dollars on the table.

Finally the plastic box was empty again. "Are you going to deal another shoe?" the gambler asked Billy.

"No, it's my break now." A Hispanic woman dealer with long red-lacquered fingernails came to stand beside Billy. And the woman who'd taken notes earlier unlocked a cash box underneath the table. Billy turned his palms upward and moved out from behind the table. He dipped his head, acknowledging the gambler or perhaps taking leave of him. He still did not look at Laura.

Without giving it any thought, she slid off the stool and followed him across the casino floor.

"Good-bye," the gambler called after her, but Laura didn't turn back. She wanted to talk to Billy, maybe even apologize. She felt as if she'd let him down and she understood by the set of his mouth and the way he was determined not to look at her that just by being there, she'd hurt him in some way. But Billy went over to two other dealers, young white men who also seemed to be off duty, and they walked through a door that said EMPLOYEES ONLY.

Laura was left alone. There were no windows in the casino and no clocks, but she was so light-headed she knew it must be the middle of the afternoon. She had to get something to eat. In one corner of the casino she saw a bar and tables, but they only served drinks, a waitress told her. "Go out over there," she said, pointing to a neon sign that said BOARDWALK.

In the hall Laura went into the ladies' room. The blister on her heel had broken, but she'd been so preoccupied she hadn't even felt it. She thought about putting on the stockings she'd bought, then dismissed the idea. That would only make it bleed. Once she was on the boardwalk, she could just take off her high heels. She could even walk on the beach if she wanted.

Suddenly she longed to be outside in the daylight. She limped to the revolving doors in the hotel lobby and was pulled around and deposited on the boardwalk. People strolled by as if it were any other day. The sun was blinding. Laura's cheeks stung and her throat felt parched. She took off her shoes and walked toward Ventnor until she came to a snack bar that opened directly onto the boardwalk. "One orangeade. And do you have any saltwater taffy?" she asked.

"Two dollars a box," said the girl who worked there. "And that'll be a dollar for the orangeade." She handed Laura her order and then sat in a folding chair next to the soft ice cream dispenser and began filing her nails.

Laura's mind leapt into a fantasy about this girl, the way it sometimes did. What Laura might have given to have changed places with her! She had curly black hair and wore a gingham uniform and false eyelashes. Laura pictured a big family. The girl and her mother were probably really close and never fought at all.

But that was as far as she got. She couldn't imagine anyone else in the family. Only the mother, who looked like an older version of the girl but with bleached blonde hair. Laura's mother had bleached her hair, too, but that was only in the past few years, when she'd begun to get gray but before she'd gotten sick and it all fell out.

Suddenly the strawberry saltwater taffy Laura was chewing felt gluey and foreign in her mouth. She climbed under the boardwalk railing onto the beach and spit it into the sand and kicked more sand on it with her foot. The beach was crowded, but the wind and the waves drowned out the sound of people. All Laura could hear was a gentle whooshing hum, that pitched and broke in her eardrums.

She walked down to the water's edge, carrying her mother's shoes in her hands. Right up close to the waves the noise was louder. When Laura began to cry, nobody could hear her. She couldn't even hear herself. But it felt good to cry. So many times when her mother was sick, other people had been crying. Her two aunts and Clara, her mother's best friend; Heather, of course, and her father. But tears rarely came to Laura's eyes. She hadn't cried at the funeral or even at the cemetery, when they lowered the casket into the ground.

About half a mile farther along the beach, when Laura was all done, she took a tissue out of her pocketbook and wiped her wet face. Streaks of beige and black were left on the tissue and it took her quite a long time to realize this was her makeup that had been on her face.

The whole day seemed ridiculous suddenly. In the clear afternoon light, the casino with its dark red walls and carpets

61

faded to a dream. She didn't understand why she'd taken so many stupid risks to gamble, nor what she'd do with the $1200 she'd won. She wasn't like those people at the slot machines; she didn't need the money.

But the gambler hadn't, either. She thought of the gold cuff links she'd seen flashing in his white shirt and the gold watch that circled his wrist. He'd still be there now, she was sure, his piles of chips before him, playing at Billy's table in the dreamlike red casino.

Billy was late for their date. Laura sat on the back porch waiting for him. She'd left all the doors in the house open so she'd hear the doorbell if it rang. She was wearing a flowered cotton dress and she'd just washed her hair. Over and over, in slow motion, she saw Billy walking away from her across the casino floor. Her heart raced; she wasn't sure if he'd come tonight or not.

Off to the side, along the hedge that separated their house from the Ruzzos', she heard a rustling. She thought it might be Billy but it was a small black dog. "Come here, puppy," Laura said, walking outside and holding out her hand.

The dog came bounding up, wagging its tail. It didn't seem to be a stray; it had a collar and some tags. "Nice puppy," said Laura. She loved animals but her parents had never let her have one.

"Is that your dog?" It was Billy's voice. Laura shook her head. He was standing on the patio behind her. She said nothing.

"Don't say hello or anything."

"How did you get in here?" asked Laura.

"I walked. You left the front door open. I know my way, anyway. Don't you remember? I used to cut the lawn once a week for your mother."

"That's right," said Laura. "Good-bye, puppy." She was using the dog now as a diversion. She was afraid of really coming face to face with Billy, of what he might say to her.

"It's okay. You don't have to look so worried." He smiled at her, a nice, friendly smile. "We're not in the casino now. We're going for a boat ride, remember? I asked you out."

Billy's car was parked around the corner. She wondered if that had to do with his not wanting his family to know they were seeing each other. He helped her into the front seat. "Wear your seat belt."

Obediently Laura fastened it. Suddenly she felt really young, like a little sister again. Billy's car was a Chevy Monza with bucket seats, and he drove it confidently, his left arm resting on the window frame. "Come on. Lighten up," he said, glancing over at her at a stoplight. "We're never going to have any fun if you keep being so serious."

He turned off Pacific and parked the car at an outdoor hamburger stand Laura had never been to. There was a tall pine tree and some picnic tables in the grass, as though it were a regular picnic area. "I'll be right back," said Billy.

Laura sat down at one of the tables, looking at the passing cars, trying to relax. Billy was acting like nothing had happened. He still liked her; she could tell by the way he was so careful with her. When they were driving, she'd reached down to turn on the radio, but he'd covered her hand with his. "Don't play that," he'd said. "Let's have quiet."

He came back to the table with both hands full. Two

cardboard trays held fried clams, Cokes, and bags of french fries drenched in cheese, the way they make them in New Jersey.

Laura didn't have the nerve to tell him she couldn't eat the clams, so she forced several into her mouth, swallowing them whole. The fries were good, though. It was the first real meal she'd eaten all day.

"Have some of my fries. I'll get more." Before Laura could stop him, Billy was gone again. They had another order of fries and Cokes, and soft ice cream hot fudge sundaes for dessert. Laura was amazed at how much she ate.

"I'm stuffed and it's your fault," she said.

"Good," said Billy. "That's what was supposed to happen."

They got back in the car and drove over to the bay side of Margate. Here the houses were big and new, and almost every driveway had a BMW or a Saab or a Mercedes in it. "Casino money," said Billy briefly and Laura didn't dare ask him to explain. She was content just to be at his side in the car, letting him decide things.

"My friend's boat is here." They'd come to a street that faced the water. Fishing boats with nets and traps were lined up between pilings, and also a few sailboats. One had a red mast and the name *John B.* written on the hull in gold letters. They walked along a dock to the boat and Billy got busy pulling sails out of boxes and adjusting the ropes.

"Take the rudder, will you? Just steer us out of the harbor, then we can cut it." He pulled a cord and the boat's small outboard engine started. Laura was used to steering. Her father once had owned a cabin cruiser with a real steering wheel that you stood in front of and spun with your hand, but when her parents got so busy with golf, they'd sold it.

Billy had raised the *John B.*'s sails and as they came into the open water of the bay, he sat beside her and turned off the engine. Suddenly there was silence. He pulled a few more ropes and the sails filled with wind. The boom began to swing around. "Look out!" he yelled, and Laura ducked.

They were moving fast now and little waves scudded against the sides of the boat. Laura was surprised by all of it. She'd never been in a sailboat before and the feeling of movement and speed without noise seemed both exhilarating and peaceful. "This is great," she told Billy. "Whose boat is it?"

"It belongs to a friend of mine, Joe Nyboris. You wouldn't know him." Next to her, Billy was holding the rudder and one of the ropes. His face looked focused and remote and it suddenly reminded Laura of the way he'd been in the casino when he was dealing blackjack.

She tilted her head and leaned against him. Billy seemed startled for a moment, then he lifted his fingers to her cheek. "You look so pretty in that dress," he said. "You look just like yourself."

"What do you mean?"

"You know . . . not like you did at Trump's. Was that makeup you had on?"

Confusion and embarrassment rose up in Laura. She leaned farther into the circle of Billy's arms. He smelled warm and salty, like the beach at midday.

For a while he didn't move. Then he turned and spun his body hard against her, catching her by surprise. They were suddenly so close! Laura could feel the bones of his chest through the thin cotton of her dress and she even thought she could feel his heart beat. His hand cupped her breast. The sailboat tilted.

"Wait . . . help! You're scaring me," cried Laura. Really, it was true. She didn't want this to happen with Billy. She didn't want it to be like with Joseph last winter.

In November, on only their second date, Joseph had taken her back to his dormitory room and they'd had sex. Laura hadn't tried to argue. Joseph had been so sure of himself and he seemed to expect it. She'd been a virgin and in the morning there was blood all over the sheets. "I'm really sorry," Joseph told her. "Girls always say they're virgins. I guess I didn't believe you." After that, they only had sex a few more times. Mainly they just necked in his car in parking lots around the city.

But Billy wasn't Joseph. Billy believed her. He moved away and with the hand that had held her breast he covered up his eyes. "Jesus, Laura, I'm sorry. What's the matter with me?"

"It's not really your fault," said Laura.

"Yes, it is. It's just . . . I keep forgetting how young you are. It's like you're another girl instead of Gabrielle's friend who was always around, running around our house in her bathing suit. Then when I saw you in the casino, it confused me even more."

"Why?"

"Are you serious? I don't know what you did to yourself, but you looked about twenty-five."

Laura grinned. "Good," she said.

"It's not good," said Billy. He grabbed her shoulders. "You could get in a lot of trouble that way. You don't know what kind of people come into the casinos. . . ."

"The boat, Billy! We're going to get turned around."

He reached for the rope and the rudder again and the wake behind them straightened. "I don't want you in the casinos. That's all."

"It's not up to you," Laura said, beginning to get her confidence back. "What is this? You think you're my father or something?"

"No," said Billy. "But if I find you anywhere near the casinos again, I guarantee he'll hear about it."

Laura laughed. "Are you saying you'll tell my father?"

"Right."

"That's it," she said. "Let's go home."

Billy continued to sail the boat. Laura crawled to the prow and considered what to do next. It was no more than a mile or two to shore. Here in the bay there was no undertow, but the water was supposed to be really polluted.

Billy was grinning at her. "What are you going to do? Jump overboard?"

"I might. You never know."

"But I do know," said Billy. "I heard what happened with you and the lifeguards."

The two of them faced each other in the tiny boat while waves gently rocked it. Billy half-stood and reached out a hand to her. "Come sit by me," he said. "You're missing the sunset."

It was true. Yellows and pinks had come into the sky and the water itself had a silvery sheen. She took Billy's hand, noticing his nails cut so square and neatly. For dealing blackjack, she thought, and she had a clear image of those hands on the cards. It was too bad she wouldn't be able to see Billy at his table in Trump Plaza again, but she could still gamble if she wanted to. There were fourteen casinos in Atlantic City and Trump's was only one.

CHAPTER
7

*Laura plunged into the ocean and swam hard, trying to
keep her bearings. It wasn't easy. Mist hid everything, even
the shoreline, but she could see by the pattern of the waves
that she was swimming more or less parallel to shore. It was
seven o'clock in the morning. No lifeguards were around
and even if they had been, they never would have seen her.*

Every once in a while she put her feet down, testing for
the bottom. Then, reassured, she swam more. Her goal was
the Ventnor Pier, about half a mile away. For three mornings in a row now, she'd made it, swimming there and back.

Laura had always been good at sports. She was fast and
graceful and if she'd cared to, she could have been an
athlete. In Laura's freshman year of high school, the gym
teacher had discovered her abilities and put her on the track

team. Laura hadn't realized in time she could just refuse, the same way she did at home with her parents.

Her event had been the broad jump and she'd tied a record among private school girls by jumping 15 feet, 7 inches in a citywide meet. She could still remember how it felt, hurtling through the air with her feet pumping. And then the moment when she landed, far beyond the others in the clean raked sand.

Swimming was nothing like that. It was monotonous and repetitive. But her body felt relaxed and totally stretched out at the end. Maybe it was swimming that had done it, because now she fell asleep every night at eleven or twelve and woke with an alert feeling at six-thirty in the morning.

Two out of three nights this week Billy had come over after he'd finished work at Trump's. He'd brought videos and they'd sat around the living room with the drapes drawn, talking and laughing, as the movies played on the VCR. Both were old comedies, *Tootsie* and *Airplane*. Laura thought Billy was probably trying to humor her out of her troubles. He'd put his arm around her on the couch and kissed her once as he left, but he'd made no other physical moves. That was fine with Laura; it meant she didn't have to decide anything right away.

The wooden pilings of the Ventnor Pier rose out of the water before her. She turned and began the long swim back. By the time she reached Marion Avenue again, the mist was beginning to rise.

Laura's stomach rumbled. Her appetite was better now, too. She ate breakfast and took a shower. Then she started her new morning routine, sitting in her mother's dressing room. First she put on underwear, then the black sundress, then her makeup, layer by layer, just the way the woman in the beauty parlor had shown her. Last of all, Laura put on her mother's gold heart necklace. This was a heart with a red ruby in the center. The ruby was surrounded by pearls, and rays extended from it as if it were the sun.

Laura had never worn any of her mother's jewelry before. Just a few weeks after her mother's death, Heather had claimed it anyway. "You don't want this stuff, do you?" she'd asked Laura, holding out three or four Chinese silk pouches where her mother had kept her bracelets and earrings, her beads and her rings. Laura had agreed. No, she didn't want that jewelry.

But the heart necklace was different. She'd found it in Ventnor, underneath a pile of silk scarves in her mother's top drawer. When Laura was a little girl, her mother had worn that necklace every day. It had been a Valentine's Day present from Laura's father. She and Heather always talked about the necklace, how romantic it was, but one day her mother had taken it off and never worn it again. After several months Laura finally asked about it. "What happened to your heart necklace?" she ventured one day in Manhattan.

"It was too big and clunky," said Laura's mother, "too 1970s. You wouldn't understand."

But to Laura, all the mystery and glamor and beauty that her mother had represented to her as a small child was in that necklace. Without it, she never seemed quite the same.

Laura looked at herself in the mirror. The necklace fit perfectly, hanging in the hollow where the bones of her throat came together. She applied more lipstick, picked up her pocketbook, and walked out the door. It was nine-thirty and she could easily have run into Billy on the sidewalk in front of their houses, but Laura was sure that would never happen. In her mind these hot July mornings, she moved in a circle of good luck, charmed and invincible.

She was on her way to Atlantic City, of course. She'd been going all week, playing blackjack in one casino after another. She'd lost nearly $400 but she didn't mind. The possibilities of the game were thrilling to her. She might win that money back in an hour; she might double or even triple it if the cards were right.

Laura got off the bus and walked over to Resorts International near the Steeplechase Pier. Merv Griffin owned this casino. His picture was in a glass box outside the entrance like a coming attraction for a movie. But the casino itself looked identical to the others she'd played in, with red velvet wallpaper and red carpets on the floors. By now Laura was comfortable in this environment. It seemed both anonymous and protective to her. After her first big win that time at Trump's, nobody had even asked for her I.D.

At this hour in the morning, on a Friday, many of the tables were empty and roped off. The crowds would come later on. Laura moved down the lines of blackjack tables, looking for a $5.00 table, preferably one with a woman dealer. The women seemed friendlier; often you could even joke with them. At last Laura found a table with an older white woman dealer. Her name tag said "Linda." She was surprisingly old, with a lined face and stylish frizzed hair. Two men in their early twenties were playing at her table, nervously kidding each other about blowing their weekend party money.

"Hi," said Laura, greeting everyone. She slid into her favorite seat, the far left-hand seat, and held out three twenty-dollar bills for chips. She'd place five-dollar bets until she started winning; then she'd up them to ten dollars. That was what the players at the high stakes tables did. Money management, it was called. Yesterday in one of the lounges at Caesar's, a craps player, slightly drunk, had explained this concept to her.

"Money management, that's the key. The odds are the odds; they won't change. In the end, it's how you play them that counts. If you're on a streak, you better put your money on the table." Then he'd leaned closer to Laura, sliding his elbow across the tiny round table in the lounge. "But I'll tell you the truth," he whispered. "I'm flat broke. This town is killing me."

Laura's first cards came to eleven. She tapped the table with her first two fingers to indicate that she'd take another card. In the casinos you weren't allowed to touch the cards or ask for more cards. If you wanted another card, you tapped your fingers; if you didn't, you waved your hand with the palm held down like a fan. At Showboat, the first day she'd played, Laura had been reprimanded by three dealers for touching the cards. Now she knew better.

All the players bet against the dealer. They bet that their cards would come closer to twenty-one than the dealer's or that the dealer would break—go over twenty-one—and they wouldn't. Each player was dealt two cards to start with, but the dealer was the only one who had a card facedown—

the dark card, it was called. In that card was the outcome of the game.

The next time around, the two other players broke and the dealer collected their chips. Laura's cards came to twenty. She waved her hand, refusing another card, and now the dealer turned over her dark card. It was a ten. Since the dealer's open card had been a seven and she was required to stand at seventeen, Laura won the hand, twenty to seventeen.

All morning the cards were in her favor. Laura played well, increasing her bets from ten to fifteen to twenty dollars a hand. By midday she'd won back her four hundred dollars and another two hundred besides. She felt exhilarated. The woman dealer, Linda, left and was replaced by an Asian man named Jack, and then by Clarice, a black woman dealer.

The game went on. The two young men—it turned out they were medical students from Ohio—lost all their money and wandered off. Other players sat down—a honeymoon couple, some Canadians on vacation, a silent, sad man from New York. Laura liked to talk while she played but some people preferred to be quiet. She could understand that, too.

In the afternoon she started to lose, and she promised herself that if she lost $200, she'd take a break. Sometimes it was good to stop, to move to another table or even another casino. But Laura let her losses go to almost $300 before she cashed in her chips and went outside. The temperature was in the nineties. On the other side of the boardwalk, the sand shimmered. Laura had to take a moment to adjust to

74

the weather. Snow could fall in July, it could be high noon or the dead of night, but inside the casino you'd never know the difference.

She bought herself a bottle of orange juice and a giant salt pretzel from a vendor and walked out to the old Steeplechase Pier to eat it. She didn't want to go far because of the heat. Her makeup already felt oily and melted on her face.

There was a high chain-link fence with a gate blocking the pier, but a covered passageway led through it. Suddenly Laura recognized where she was. Her family sometimes came here to take the helicopter to New York. The summer she was twelve, Laura and her mother had gone to the city every other Tuesday, back and forth on the helicopter in one day, so that Laura could get her braces adjusted.

She'd loved it then, always taking a window seat. But this summer, though her father had told her she could take the helicopter and come to New York whenever she was lonely, it seemed impossible. She was certain the helicopter would crash, that it would fall out of the sky like a rock dropped from a rooftop.

Laura sat down to eat her lunch on a bench that had been provided for passengers. But the moment she unwrapped her pretzel, a man in a blue mechanic's jumpsuit appeared. "You can't stay here, Miss. This is a helicopter landing."

"I know that," said Laura.

"You'll have to move."

"I'm not bothering anyone." She opened her orange juice and began drinking it in a slow, exaggerated fashion. Some stubbornness about rules and bureaucracy and being told what to do seized her and she became completely immovable.

"I don't think you heard me," said the man.

Laura turned away from him, but he surprised her by hitting her elbow suddenly and knocking the orange juice out of her hand. It splattered across both of them. "I told you to move. Now move." His voice was soft, almost conversational.

Laura stood up and left. Tears came into her eyes, outrage at the way she'd been treated, but she had no intention of crying. Blindly she walked up the boardwalk, away from the pier and the casino at Resorts. Her day of gambling had been spoiled. She opened her pocketbook and touched the crisp hundred-dollar bills inside. What did she want with them, anyway? She felt like throwing them into the trash.

A weekend crowd was on the boardwalk. Tourists with cameras and bathing suits passed her on either side, and a motorized tram with about twenty people in it rolled by smoothly on its rubber wheels. Right behind it, unbelievably, she saw Gabrielle Ruzzo walking toward her. She seemed so out of place in Atlantic City that Laura hardly knew what to do.

"Laura! How great! What are you doing here?" Gabrielle took her arm and changed directions to walk with her.

Laura held up her pretzel, half-eaten. "Having lunch."

"That's no lunch," said Gabrielle. "Come on. I'll take you to a great place. I've been meaning to call you, but you wouldn't believe how busy I've been. Perfect timing. . . . I'm on my break now." She turned off the boardwalk at a big white building jutting into the sea. "It's right here. This way."

Laura followed Gabrielle up an escalator and past a row of small shops. The building they were in was a shopping mall made to look like an ocean liner. "Ocean I," it was called. Laura had seen it many times, but she'd never been inside. At the end of the second floor was a cafeteria and a group of tables. "Stay here," said Gabrielle. "What would you like? They have great salads and frozen yogurt. . . ."

"Frozen yogurt sounds good." Suddenly Laura felt exhausted, but maybe it was just hunger. She waited for Gabrielle to come back, idly looking into the window of a shop filled with lacy underwear.

"Really, seriously . . . What are you doing in A.C.?" Gabrielle put two trays in front of them. Little plastic containers held strawberry frozen yogurt, topped with nuts and fruit.

"Shopping," said Laura. "I need some new underwear and something nice to wear, a dress maybe. My father's coming tonight and he said he'd take us to one of the shows at the casinos."

"Us?"

"Heather and me." The yogurt was good. It slid coolly down her throat.

"I didn't know Heather was here. My mother's seen you walking back and forth from the beach in the morning, but she's never seen Heather. She says you must be going swimming because your hair's wet on the way back."

That was typical. Mrs. Ruzzo knew everything that happened on Marion Avenue.

"Heather's been staying in New York," Laura said. "She's got a lot to do. She's getting married next month."

"Married! To who?"

"Some man named Leo Kramer. He's a lawyer."

"Poor guy," Gabrielle said. Through the years she'd picked up Laura's own feelings about Heather. When they were younger, about thirteen or fourteen, they'd called Heather "the Bitch" or just "B" for short.

"But what about you? What are you going to do all summer?" Gabrielle grabbed Laura's wrist. "You can't stay in that house alone."

"I've been doing it, haven't I? My father doesn't mind so you shouldn't worry about it, either." Laura smiled to soften the effect of her words. She didn't want to hurt Gabrielle's feelings again. "For one thing, I've been doing a lot of swimming, working on my physical fitness. You should see my arm muscles. No one's going to mess with me."

"Can I ask you something? I don't mean to be rude or anything, but how come you have so much makeup on?"

"Just an experiment," said Laura. "What do you think?"

"It makes you look older." Gabrielle pushed her yogurt away and stood up. "Come on. I still have half an hour. I'll go shopping with you if you want."

Laura and Gabrielle went into the lingerie shop and crowded into a dressing room to watch Laura try on some slips and strapless bras.

"I like this push-up one," Laura said. "It'll look good with low necklines." She put her regular bra and her sundress back on. "How's your brother Billy?"

"Billy? What do you want to know about him for?"

"I don't know. Just curious." Laura looked around the store. They were waiting for the salesgirl to ring up the bill.

"I don't really see him much," Gabrielle said. "He's gone in the morning and then I don't get off work until ten. Lots of nights I go out with Greg, so by the time I get home all of them are asleep."

"You mean you never talk to Billy at all?" asked Laura.

"Not really. My mother thinks he's seeing someone because he's been acting really happy lately but she doesn't think it's serious because he's always in by midnight. What is this? Do you have a crush on my brother?"

"How could I? I've hardly even seen him since I was fourteen." Laura took out a hundred-dollar bill to pay the check.

"God, Laura! Don't you have anything smaller?"

"No. This is all my father gave me."

They took the escalator down to a shop that Gabrielle knew about. It sold only silk clothing, in brilliant colors. Laura chose a flared fuchsia skirt and a midnight blue top with spaghetti straps. She imagined herself in Trump's, walking over to Billy, while the silk fabric picked up the casino lights. "Your sister helped me buy this," she'd say. "Do you like it?"

And when he reached for her, touching her bare shoulder while all the players at his blackjack table watched, she'd stop him and say, "Your sister says you're seeing somebody right now, but nobody thinks it's serious. True or false? Tell me the truth. True or false?"

CHAPTER
8

In the end only Heather showed up on Friday night. Laura's father had business in New York that "couldn't wait."

"Something about a tax audit . . ." said Heather. "He may come for the day Sunday, but you know what that means. Don't count on it, in other words."

Danny Samuels owned a men's dress shirt company. The showroom was in New York but the factory was in North Carolina. Throughout Heather's and Laura's childhood he'd worked evenings and sometimes weekends. "He's a workaholic," claimed Heather when she'd learned the word in college. "That's not true, Heather," said their mother. "If he didn't work those hours, you wouldn't have the nice things you do. He's got to compete with Hong Kong. Do you know how many manufacturers like your father have gone out of business?"

But according to Heather, Danny Samuels was working harder than ever now. It was her theory that he was using the business to console himself after their mother's death. "Look, Laura, believe me. I'm in New York living with him. He won't talk about her at all. And no matter what time it is, he's at the dining room table working—in the middle of the night, at six in the morning. I swear he doesn't sleep."

"I wish he'd come to Ventnor," said Laura. "I really wanted to see him."

Expecting her father, Laura had worn her new silk top with jeans and put on more makeup. After all, part of the reason she was changing herself was for him. "You're such a pretty girl but nobody would ever know it," he'd commented a few times last summer. "Talk to Heather or your mother, I'm sure they'd be glad to show you what to do."

Tonight when she'd heard the taxi pull up to the curb, Laura had come running from the house. Marion Avenue was deserted but sprinklers were on and she could hear the shouts of children. The taxi door slammed, but only Heather got out. "Could you take my bag?" she said. "Daddy isn't coming."

Heather had two pieces of luggage and she was wearing a black jumpsuit. A diamond engagement ring sparkled on her left hand.

"Where did you get that ring?" Laura asked. "You didn't have it last time."

"It was Leo's grandmother's but we took it to a jeweler to have it reset. Do you like it?"

"Yes," said Laura truthfully. "It's beautiful."

Heather peered at Laura. "You've changed, too, since last time. Have you been using Mommy's makeup or what?"

"This is my own makeup. I bought it."

"Oh?" said Heather. "That's good, I think. It's a step forward."

Suddenly a car horn honked at them from the street. It was Mrs. Ruzzo, turning into her driveway. She rolled down the car window. "Is that you, Heather? We haven't seen you all summer."

Heather walked over to the curb again, followed by Laura. "I've only been coming weekends. How is everyone?"

"Fine, we're all fine. I've been telling your sister she should come over more often. Gabrielle's working in A.C.—I'm sure Laura's told you—but I'm home. You girls should both come over. Come for Sunday dinner, why don't you?"

"That sounds great," said Heather. "What time?"

"At about three-thirty? Billy has the day off so you'll have a chance to see him again, and if I call Marna and tell her you're coming, maybe she'll come, too." She grabbed Heather's hand. "What's this I see?"

"I'm engaged. I'm getting married in September."

"Oh, Heather, how wonderful for your father! What a good time for a piece of good news! On Sunday you'll tell us all about it."

"God, Heather, why did you have to do that?" Laura said the moment Mrs. Ruzzo's car disappeared into her garage.

"Do what?"

"Say we'd come without even asking me. You always do that. You never ask my opinion about anything." She went into the house and slammed the door, leaving Heather and her bag outside.

Heather opened the front door slowly. "Take it easy, Laura. I'm sorry, okay? I thought you'd *want* to have Sunday dinner there. You used to spend all your time at the Ruzzos. Last summer, as I remember, we hardly saw you."

"You still shouldn't have said we'd go without asking me," Laura said stubbornly. There was no way she was going to sit through dinner at the Ruzzos with Billy, answering everyone's questions with lies.

Heather held up her hands. "Okay, okay. I'll call Mrs. Ruzzo and say we're not coming."

"Fine," said Laura. "When?"

"Right now. God, you always have to have your own way, don't you?" Heather raced past Laura up the stairs and Laura heard her picking up the phone. "No, we can't come. . . . Laura made other plans. Right, definitely. . . . me, too. 'Bye."

Laura slid her hand up and down the smooth golden wood of the bannister, waiting until Heather might have calmed down. "Thanks a lot, Heather, for doing that," she said when she came into her sister's room.

"Anything for you." Heather sighed. Laura couldn't tell if she was being sarcastic or not. "I'm really exhausted, though. My body feels like a truck ran over it."

"You're not sick, are you?" Anxiety rose up in Laura and she studied her sister's neck and throat for swollen glands.

"I don't think so. I probably just need some exercise. I sit in those N.Y.U. classrooms all morning, crammed into those ridiculous desks, writing until my arm feels like it'll fall off."

"What's school like?" Laura asked. "You never say anything about it."

Heather shrugged. "It's okay, I guess. To tell you the truth, I'd rather just be with Leo. Just be married, I mean. But I've come this far."

"No. Don't stop," said Laura. "It's good that you'll be a lawyer."

"You really think so?"

"Sure. It's important to have a profession."

It surprised Laura that her opinion seemed to matter to Heather. Maybe they could actually have a nice weekend. She remembered another summer evening many years ago—it must have been the first time their parents had left them alone in the house. When it grew dark, Laura had become frightened and yet she'd known her sister would take care of her.

"I'd better change my clothes." Heather got out of her jumpsuit and put on pleated shorts and a shirt. "Are our bikes still here?"

"I don't know. You want to go look?"

They found their bicycles, good ten-speed bikes that their parents had bought them just two years before, against the back wall of the garage. The paint was still shiny, Heather's gold and Laura's silver, once they'd dusted the fenders off. "But the tires need air," Heather said. "And we need to get something to eat."

She handed Laura the bicycle pump and went into the house. When she returned, she put a package of Oreos and two small containers of apple juice into the bike baskets. Laura had the bikes in the driveway, propped up on their kickstands.

"Where should we go?" asked Laura.

"Lucy the Elephant?"

"Fine."

It was dinnertime. The boardwalk and the beach were almost empty as Heather and Laura rode along, the wheels of their bicycles clicking. Two joggers passed them and in the backyards on the other side of the boardwalk they could see an old man tending his tomato plants, a big family assembled for a barbecue, a couple lying on two chaise longues, holding hands across the space between them. "That's Leo and me in twenty years," Heather said.

"Do you really love him?" asked Laura.

"Yes, I do."

Laura was silent. She couldn't imagine feeling like that, especially about someone as plain and ordinary as Leo.

The boardwalk ended, but a ramp led down to the street. Now they were in Margate, a town that was uniformly richer than Ventnor and known for having more Jews. Her mother had wanted to move here, but Laura's father refused. "Why should we when we have your parents' house?" he had said. "But I didn't choose it," her mother had answered. Two summers later they put Laura's grandparents into a nursing home and her mother redecorated the entire downstairs.

"Stop," said Heather. She signaled with her left hand and they turned into a grassy park. It was the home of Lucy the Elephant, and here she was, six stories high, a painted tin elephant towering above them.

Lucy had been built during the 1880s. Originally she was one of three elephants put up by the town of Margate to attract visitors. There was a stairway inside her, and when Heather and Laura were little, they'd loved to climb to the top and emerge beneath Lucy's canopy, a curved and delicate structure like a pagoda. But by the time they were teenagers Lucy had become just a place to go. They'd ride there on bikes with their friends or else when they wanted to get out of the house.

Now, in the evening, there was no one visiting Lucy. The bleachers outside her little park were empty. Heather and Laura wheeled their bikes over to them and sat down. Heather divided up the Oreos, six for each of them, democratically, the way they had as children, and handed Laura one of the apple juices.

Sea gulls wheeled in the sky and tiny sandpipers pecked in the sand near their feet. For a long time neither sister spoke, and then Heather asked, "Do you think about Mommy?"

"I knew you were going to ask me that."

Heather tossed a piece of an Oreo onto the ground for the birds. "I miss her so much. If I didn't have Leo, I don't know what I'd do."

"Well, I don't have Leo. I don't really have anyone," said Laura shortly. More birds were gathering now, waiting for cookies. Laura threw them her last two Oreos. She knew she couldn't eat them now.

"You have me," said Heather. "And Daddy, too, of course."

"Anyway, it's different for me," Laura went on. "I never was as close to Mommy as you were."

Heather moved nearer to Laura on the bleachers until their bodies were touching. "That's what Leo says. He says that because you two didn't get along, that only makes her death harder for you."

"Look," said Laura. "Why don't you let me decide how I feel? You don't have to worry about me. I'm busy every day. I swim, I take walks." Laura turned away and thought, *Yes, and I go to the casinos pretending to be you. I play blackjack and I've won fifteen hundred dollars so far. Billy Ruzzo has trouble keeping his hands off me. . . .*

"I guess it's better for you to work things out your own way," Heather said. She stood up and the birds scattered into the sky. "Maybe you need to mourn alone."

"Maybe I don't need to mourn at all," said Laura.

"That's ridiculous. She was your mother and you loved her and now she's dead. Not that she couldn't be weird sometimes. . . .

"You know what I was thinking of the other day? Remember how Mommy would try to teach us table manners at dinner? I'd do what she said, of course, but you'd just sit there, eating any way you wanted. 'Uh-huh,' you'd say, but you never really listened.

"Mommy would get so frustrated. One time, we were probably, like, eight and thirteen, and she suddenly reached over and jabbed the back of your hand with her fork."

"Right," said Laura. "I remember that."

Heather's hair was in a ponytail and she took off the elastic and put it back to tighten her hair against the wind. "But it didn't hurt, did it? She wanted us to have good manners, that's all. Then when we went out, like to a restaurant or something, we wouldn't embarrass ourselves."

"Her, you mean."

"What?" asked Heather.

"She didn't want us to embarrass her."

"I think you're wrong."

Laura said, "You don't know. I was the embarrassing one, not you. Nothing I ever did was right."

"That's not true," said Heather.

"Yeah, sure," said Laura. "Tell me one thing that I did that was right—once I was no longer a cute adorable little baby, I mean."

"There were plenty of times . . ." Heather kicked at the sand, then dug her toes into it. "She was always talking about you to her friends, telling them the things you'd done. Like . . . well, she was really proud of you when you were on the track team that time."

"Track? Why would she care about track?" But as soon as she said the words, Laura knew the reason. She'd won her event. It was a public achievement. A familiar bitter feeling came into her throat and her stomach felt tight and hollow.

Her face must have changed, too, because suddenly Heather sat down on the bleachers again and took her hand. "That's right. Cry. You need to cry."

Laura started sobbing. She felt really sad and desperate but she knew she could never explain why. It was easiest just to let Heather think she missed their mother. The beach wind blew at her tears, sending them sideways on her face in streams.

"Poor Laura," said Heather. She wheeled Laura's bike over to her. "Here. Let's go home," she said.

The whole weekend was like that, with Heather treating Laura as if she were recovering from an illness. On Saturday night they made fudge and swam in the surf. That was Laura's idea. Actually Heather was terrified of the dark water. On Sunday morning they swam again, to the Ventnor Pier and back with Heather trailing behind and finally giving up and walking along the beach.

Heather cooked their meals and insisted on buying Laura groceries for the week, going down the aisles of the supermarket and choosing bland, healthy foods like cottage cheese and shredded wheat and bananas. The delivery boy brought them to the back door.

"But I can't believe you're not bored out of your mind here," Heather said to Laura. She was standing on a kitchen chair and putting the groceries away in the cupboard.

"I'm different than you. I don't need to keep busy to be happy," said Laura.

In a different mood Heather might have challenged this, but the weekend seemed to have relaxed her. Her face was slightly tanned and she'd been wearing Laura's old clothes and going barefoot in the house.

"Still," Heather said, getting down, "You have to do *something* with your days."

For a moment, Laura wanted more than anything to tell her sister about the casinos. But she warned herself to keep quiet. Once or twice after she started high school, she'd told Heather secrets—that she'd cut school, say, or driven around in someone's car. But in subtle ways, Heather had used the information against her, hinting to their parents that Laura couldn't be trusted.

"It's almost four-thirty. Are you going to take the same helicopter as last weekend?" Laura asked.

"God! I'd better hurry. Do you have any pads? I think I'm getting my period."

"In my top drawer. I'll wait for you here." She walked out onto the screened porch. The air was close and there was a slight smell of mildew from the cushions on the porch furniture. Laura sat on the glider against the back wall and stared into the garden.

She began swinging on the glider, back and forth, enjoying the regular creaking of the runners at the bottom. She could almost hypnotize herself sometimes, watching leaves or clouds or just listening to a sound, closing out everything else. Back and forth on the glider, creak slide, creak slide. When Heather came onto the porch, Laura didn't know it until the glider stopped. She was flung forward, almost onto the floor. Heather had jammed the mechanism with her foot.

"What's this?" her sister screamed, sticking her wallet into Laura's face, almost slapping her with it. "I can't believe it! I go into your drawer and this is what I find!" The wallet was open and Laura could see money sticking out and the credit cards lined up in their little pockets.

"Explain what you were doing with my wallet," ordered Heather. "And it had better be good."

The words were familiar to Laura. For years she'd heard them from both her parents whenever she'd been caught doing anything wrong. But now, as then, she wasn't inclined to explain.

"So am I to gather you're a thief now, too?" Heather sat on the glider, but at the other end. She did not look at Laura. Her face was damp with sweat.

"I didn't spend any of your money," said Laura. "Go ahead. Count it."

"Then why did you take my wallet?"

"I didn't. I found it in your room, under your bed. I was going to send it back Express Mail, but I forgot to."

"Do you expect me to believe that?" Heather asked, standing up. "I don't think Daddy will."

A panic, quite real this time, seized Laura and she grabbed her sister's arm. "No, please, don't tell Daddy," she pleaded. "I don't want him to get mad at me. I couldn't stand that. Besides," she added, "don't you think he has enough to worry about?"

"Maybe. We'll see." Heather pocketed the wallet and wiped her upper lip with her fingers. "Come upstairs," she ordered Laura. "I need help packing. I don't want to miss the helicopter."

"God forbid."

"What? I didn't hear you. What did you say?"

"Nothing," said Laura.

She waited until it was getting dark, wanting the darkness to hide her. But when she stepped from the house in her silk skirt and top and a black short-sleeved sweater of her mother's, Laura saw Billy's red Monza at the curb. The door was open and the light was on and he was sitting inside listening to the radio.

Laura approached the car, not meaning to but drawn by the music. It was a slow rock and roll song, but the words about mothers crying and their sons dying didn't seem to fit.

"Laura!" Billy turned to face her.

"What song is that?" she asked.

"Marvin Gaye. 'What's Goin' On?' "

"Not much. Heather was here for the weekend."

"No, I meant that's the name of the song, 'What's Goin' On?' " He turned off the radio. In the silence, Laura could hear the sea pounding. It was always louder at night.

"Where are you going?" Billy asked.

"To the synagogue." It was the first thing that came into Laura's mind. So what if services were Friday night, not Sunday night? Billy wouldn't know that.

"The one on Melbourne?"

Laura nodded.

"I'd give you a ride, but I told my mother I'd take Marna back to Camden tonight. Her husband had to work."

Laura put her fingers on Billy's wrist. "That's okay. It's only ten blocks from here and I was planning to walk. See, I'm wearing low heels." She stepped back to show him.

"Uh huh. I like your red skirt, too."

"It's not red, it's fuchsia," Laura said. "Your sister helped me buy it."

"It's nice." Billy got out and closed the door to his car. "I better go now."

"Can you come over tomorrow after work?"

Billy leaned toward her and his lips brushed her cheek. "You got it," he said.

Laura watched him walk up his driveway. Then she went to the corner and waited for the bus to Atlantic City.

CHAPTER
9

She hadn't planned to go to Trump's and she hadn't meant to look for the gambler who'd been at Billy's table. Yet the first casino she came to when she got off the bus was Trump's and the only blackjack table she saw when she walked into the casino was Billy's. It was halfway across the room but she saw it anyway.

"Ah," said the gambler. "There you are." In a dark suit and a red silk tie, he looked as elegant and perfect as he had before. When Laura approached, he rose to greet her. "Please sit down."

Laura's heart pounded but she tried to appear calm. It was the first time she'd been in a casino without Heather's I.D. and she had the feeling she shouldn't gamble or call attention to herself in any way. Therefore, a few minutes later, when the waitress came over to take drink orders, she shook her head. "You must have something," said the gambler. "Two Scotch and waters," he told the waitress.

She looked Laura over with her pencil poised. Laura stared back, knowing it would be more revealing to look away. The waitress was interchangeable with all the other cocktail waitresses at all the other casinos. Her costume was black satin, cut like a bathing suit, and she wore black fishnet stockings and black spike heels. Her eyelashes were so long that they couldn't possibly be real.

"What are you waiting for?" the gambler asked the waitress. She wrote down the order and disappeared.

"So," said the gambler, "I thought I'd see you again last Sunday, but you never came back." He was playing three hands of blackjack again, placing his green twenty-five-dollar chips on the table in an almost bored way. His hand motions were bored, too, a slight tap with his index finger for another card, a single side movement of his fingers, refusing.

"Aren't you going to play?" he asked Laura, laying out two purple chips for more green ones. They were the only people at the table, and the dealer, a small Asian woman named Ping, looked at Laura inquiringly.

"Not right now. I think I'll just watch you." Laura knew she could not have concentrated with the gambler sitting next to her. She looked down. The worsted fabric of his pants was creased in a perfectly straight line and his black tasseled loafers reflected the light. Her heart beat hard, but more slowly than before. "What's your name?" she asked him. It was her first question to the gambler and she chided herself for being dumb enough to ask it.

"Ari Hassan."

"Oh, I thought you were from a foreign country."

"I am. I'm from Lebanon."

"Lebanon." All Laura could think of was a restaurant her parents had taken her to called The Cedars of Lebanon, a dark room with sweet, exotic food.

"Bets, gentlemen," said the dealer. Two other men had sat down at the table. They were close to her father's age and by their looks and manner could have been friends of his, men he'd do business with or greet at the synagogue. One had rimless glasses and was smoking a long, thin cigar; the other was bald and wore a tuxedo and a white, pleated shirt.

Ari continued to play three hands for fifty dollars each; the others played only one but were betting with black hundred-dollar chips.

"You sure you won't play?" Ari asked Laura. She shook her head. She was still too nervous. Besides, the high rollers were at this table and she wanted to watch them. The atmosphere was totally different from the five-dollar tables in the other casinos. There you could see people literally sweat as they lost money, or bow their heads, appearing to be broken. She knew no players would ever bow their heads at Billy's table.

Ping, the dealer, was pretty and after a few minutes the two older men began to flirt with her and tease her. She didn't really respond but a smile stayed on her mouth.

"Listen, baby, you better start giving me better cards than these," said the man in the tuxedo after he'd broken twice in a row.

"I need a ten. Hit me with a ten," demanded the other. "Do you like gold? Diamonds? I'm in the jewelry business, I can get you whatever you want."

But the luck of both men was bad and though they pushed more and more black chips onto the table, the dealer kept picking them up. At last one of the men took out his wallet and counted the bills inside. "This broad won't give us good cards no matter what," he said loudly to his friend. "The hell with it. We'll find another one who will." Then he turned to Ari. "How come you keep hitting? What's your secret?"

"I think it is her," Ari said, nodding at Laura.

She laughed self-consciously. "But I haven't done anything."

"Just the way your hands are holding on to the edge of the table. That can be enough."

Ping left and the new dealer, a young black man named Jeffrey, conferred with the pit boss. Laura looked down at her hands, tanned and narrow, with pale pink nail polish. "Can I move them?" she asked.

"I'd rather you didn't. Well, perhaps you could move one at a time."

There was nothing humorous in Ari's tone; she realized he meant what he said. "But really, how can you expect me to keep my hands in the same position all night? I don't even have to stay here."

"Of course, but I am enjoying your company and it is

still early—only ten." Ari picked up five hundred-dollar chips and handed them to her. "Please stay."

"Are you paying me?" Laura asked in a low voice. The waitress had come back for more drink orders and was looking at them curiously. This time when Laura refused a drink, Ari did not press her.

With his own hands, he closed her hand around the small pile of chips. She was left with an impression of delicacy and power. "I only want you to enjoy yourself, to play blackjack with me. Now it's nighttime. Outside, the dark Atlantic Ocean is falling onto the shore and the sand on the beach is cold. But here in the casino everything is warm. More than warm! Tonight the cards are hot!"

Laura was unable to argue with him. She felt mesmerized, nearly helpless. She held onto the table with one hand and pushed one of the chips Ari had given her toward the dealer. "May I have twenty fives for this?"

She bet the way she always did, taking cards on intuition, hoping the dealer would break or come up short, but Ari stopped her after only two hands. "This six should have come to you," he said. "You're interfering with my cards." On Sunday night the casino was not crowded and no one else had come to play at the table.

"*Your* cards?"

"Certainly." He placed two twenty-five-dollar chips in each of his three positions. "When you play incorrectly, when you don't take a card when you should or take one when you shouldn't, you change everyone else's cards, too."

Laura fanned her fingers, letting the dealer know she wouldn't be betting this time. She was wearing her mother's

98

gold heart necklace and she put her hand over it and slid the heart back and forth, an inch or two along the chain. "How come nobody else I ever played with said this to me?"

"Probably too polite," said Ari. "You might have noticed people leaving the table, though." The waitress had brought his drink and he swirled the ice around in the glass. "How long have you been playing blackjack?"

"A week."

"Well, then the answer's simple. It's time for you to learn how." He smiled at her and began breaking his piles of twenty-five-dollar chips into stacks of eight. There were twelve of these when he was done, arrayed before him like a fortress. Twelve times two hundred made twenty-four hundred dollars, calculated Laura.

"I'll take five hundreds, please," Ari told the dealer. "And hundreds for the extra four."

The pit boss had to come over then to count the chips and authorize the transaction. Ari leaned back on his stool, released for the moment from the table's pull. "Will you have dinner with me?" he asked Laura.

"Yes," she said simply.

Ari guided her by the elbow out of the casino to the bank of elevators in the lobby. When the brass doors of one closed and it began to rise, Laura was amazed to see the lights of other buildings fall rapidly away. The elevator had a glass wall, but before she could get her bearings or understand it, Ari was leading her out.

"Please . . ." said Laura. They had just passed a ladies' room. "I'll be right back." Inside she rushed over to the mirror to look at herself. She was so flattered and excited by Ari's interest in her that she could hardly focus on her own face. She blotted her cheeks with a wet paper towel and put on more lipstick and ran her brush through her hair. Then as an afterthought, she unbuttoned her mother's black sweater so that Ari would see her electric blue chemise and the top of her breasts, pushed up by the strapless bra.

The restaurant they went to was called Ivana's. It was dim and soft and sparkling, lit by candles and tiny spotlights on vases of flowers. Inside, the maître d', wearing a white shirt and tails, greeted Ari by name. "Ah, Mr. Hassan. We were hoping to see you tonight. A table for two?" He led them to a corner table and pulled out Laura's chair with a flourish. Everything this man did seemed dramatic. "May I get you something to drink? Wine, perhaps?"

"A split of champagne," said Ari.

"Very good." The maître d' bowed and disappeared.

Ari unfolded his linen napkin and put it on his lap, keeping his eyes on Laura. She decided not to smile, but only looked back at him. Her cheeks felt hot, almost as if she had a fever. "You must tell me your name," said Ari.

"Oh, I'm sorry. I'm Heather Samuels." Even though she had nothing now to prove she was Heather, Laura was more comfortable with her sister's name. Like the makeup and clothing she wore, it was a disguise, something to conceal her and keep her safe. Uneasily she remembered the way Ari's hands had closed around hers when he'd made her keep the chips.

His skin was dark, not like her own when it tanned in summer, but with a darkness that went deep beneath the surface cells. He had a broad forehead, a straight nose, and long, narrow lips. He did not smile often, and when he did, she felt as if he were measuring her. "Will you tell me now what I did wrong? When I was playing blackjack, I mean."

A waiter had brought the champagne in a silver bucket and a single small orchid for Laura. "It's something they give you here," said Ari. "You don't have to wear it."

"He smiled and raised his glass in a kind of mock toast. "I prefer not to talk about cards at dinner, but afterward, if you like, I'll explain to you the system I use to play."

"Those two men," said Laura, "were they using it, too?"

"Of course. Otherwise I would have left the table. It's far from a secret, you know." He held up the menu and began to describe the dishes to her.

In the end he ordered for them both, veal which came on a big warm plate with a lemon sauce and potatoes and vegetables. It was the first meat Laura had eaten since last summer. She thought it was delicious.

Without really noticing it, she'd drunk a lot of champagne, too. Drinking wasn't something Laura was used to; a few times with Joseph she'd had wine or some beers at a student bar and it had made her head swim. But now the champagne only seemed to free her. She was able to ask Ari questions without worrying about what he'd think and in this way she learned about him.

Although he was born in Lebanon, he'd come to the United States with his mother and a younger brother when he was only seven. An uncle had sent for them after his father had been killed in a border skirmish. He'd grown up in Queens and had never been back to his own country.

To her question about work, he would say only that he was "in business."

Every Sunday afternoon Ari took a limousine to Atlantic City to play blackjack; he'd been doing it for several years. He stayed until Tuesday morning, always gambling at Trump's at the table where Laura had found him.

"Do you get to know the dealers?" she asked, thinking of Billy.

"I make it a practice not to speak to them. It's bad luck."

"You're superstitious!"

Ari did not smile. "Whatever works."

They were waiting for their coffee. Laura drank the last inch of champagne in her glass. "I want to thank you for taking me to dinner. And for the chips, too." They were in the bottom of her pocketbook now, four black hundred-dollar chips.

"You can thank Donald Trump for the dinner. It costs me nothing."

"What? Why?"

"I'm comped. The casino pays my bills."

"Even your room?"

Ari nodded. "They give me a line of credit in the casino. As long as they see that I'm spending the money, several thousand each time, they're glad to pay. They want me to come back, you see. Clean towels and a comfortable bed, food, a little champagne, an orchid for a pretty companion—what is it to them? Nothing. Less than nothing."

Laura looked around the restaurant. Even at this hour, several tables were full and the people who were eating all seemed sophisticated and at ease. "What about them? Are they comped, too?"

"Probably. At least the one who signs for the bill is."

A waiter brought their coffee, each in a little silver pot, and wheeled a dessert tray over. "Try this. It's delicious," said Ari, handing Laura a meringue filled with chocolate cream. But he took nothing for himself.

"Now tell me how you play blackjack. You promised."

Ari poured himself coffee and put four sugar cubes in it. "Black and sweet is best," he said. "All right. It's really very simple. You play the way the dealer does. If the dealer has a seven or over, you draw to seventeen. If he has a six or under, you only draw to twelve. You wait for him to break."

"You mean I'm betting that he will?"

He nodded. "You must always assume that the dark card is a ten." Laura wanted to ask why, but Ari held up his hand, stopping her. "It's the odds, you see. There are twelve face cards and four tens in every deck, eight decks in a shoe—sixteen times eight is a hundred and twenty-eight tens. And that's out of only four hundred and sixteen cards all together.

"Now there's something else, too. Doubling down. When you've got two cards totaling nine, ten, or eleven and you see that the dealer's top card is a three, a four, or a five you should always double down."

Laura knew what he meant. She'd also seen players divide their cards and increase their bets in the middle of a hand, but she'd never known when to do it herself. A wave of embarrassment came over her. She remembered a fat man at Caesar's glaring at her as he pulled his bulk off the stool after only one hand. "Someone should teach you to play cards. Either that or stop you at the door," he'd said. At the time Laura had thought he was annoyed at losing a fifty-dollar bet.

"Don't look so upset," said Ari. "You'll be fine now. You'll win a lot of money." He signed the bill and they left the restaurant, ushered to the door by the maître d', who acted as if he'd been their host at a wonderful party.

The dealer Ping was back at Billy's table but only one place was available. "You take it," Laura said and she put both her hands on the edge of the table for Ari.

For more than an hour she watched him play blackjack and she saw that it was true—he never deviated from his system. When he was winning, he bet heavily; when he was losing, he held back. "Money management, it's as simple as that," echoed a voice in her head.

At last Ari made her play. "Where are your chips? Put them on the table." He watched her open her purse. "There's nothing to be nervous about."

It was like another game. The knowledge that she would always draw according to the dealer's cards removed a degree of suspense and intuiton for Laura. Even after she'd lost several hands, her stomach didn't hurt. She held her mother's gold heart necklace in her hand as she watched the cards fan down to her. She understood Ari's superstition better now; there was nothing to decide.

She lost nearly the entire $500, then slowly built it up again. By the time she'd won a hundred more it was two o'clock in the morning. "Here," she told Ari, pushing over all but four of her twenty-five-dollar chips. "It's time for me to go home."

"Don't be silly. Look how much you've helped me win tonight." He drew back his arm to show Laura his chips, all hundreds now, leaning toward each other in high towers. Then he handed her five of them. "Will you come and see me tomorrow night again?"

She nodded.

"You'll be all right, I think. The valets in front will find you a cab." Laura had told him that she lived on Marion Avenue in Ventnor; she didn't mention that she also lived in New York.

Ari stood as she rose. His manners were old-fashioned, more like her grandfather's than her father's, she thought. "You'd better button your sweater," he said. "It might be cold outside."

He smiled as he watched her, and her fingers shook a little because the buttonholes were tiny.

"Good night. And thanks again for everything." Laura turned to go.

"Your sweater . . ." said Ari.

She looked down. She'd buttoned it wrong. One side was two inches longer than the other. "See what you do to me," she said to him. She meant this to sound light and flirtatious, but because he didn't respond, the words stayed in the air between them until she walked away.

CHAPTER
10

Billy loved old music. He'd made tapes from 1950s jazz and rock records, of love songs and bebop tunes, and on Monday night he played one for Laura. They were driving in his car, just driving in the evening down the swampy New Jersey shore, and he pulled a small tape player from under his seat.

"Try this," he told Laura, inserting a tape and pushing the play button. He handed her the machine and pulled down his sun visor against the setting sun. It was a hot misty evening without any view. The swamp birds were clustering on telephone wires.

As each song came on, Billy said its name and the name of the group. "Sincerely," by the Moonglows. "Earth

Angel," by the Penguins. "In the Still of the Night," by the Five Satins. To Laura the words to the songs were sentimental and the music was so slow it seemed almost to be playing at the wrong speed, but she didn't tell Billy that.

She was happy to be with him. All she had to do was laugh and smile and sometimes lean her head against his shoulder as he drove—Billy liked her no matter what. It wasn't like it was with Ari, when she tried to be careful of every word, balancing on a tightrope, waiting to see if she'd fall.

Even thinking about Ari made her stomach turn over. She already had her clothes laid out at home, Heather's blue silk shirt and white silk pants and her mother's patent leather pumps. When Billy took her back, she'd have to get dressed fast and call a cab so she'd get to Trump's by ten or ten-thirty. It was so strange. Billy had left there only an hour ago; probably he'd been face to face with Ari for most of his shift. Laura resisted a temptation to ask him about Ari. When the tape ended, she said, "Did you have a destination in mind? I mean, where are we going?"

He smiled. "There's a drive-in movie in Palermo. I thought we could pick up a six-pack and see a double feature."

"A double feature! That's too long," Laura said. "I know I'll never be able to stay up for that. Besides, do you even know what's playing?"

"Probably something you've been dying to see, like *Rocky IV* or *The Terminator*."

"Billy!" She pretended to give his shoulder a punch. They

were coming into Ocean City. Laura had been here a few times last summer with Gabrielle and some of her friends; it wasn't much, just another sandbar town.

Billy stopped at a package store and came out with a six-pack, a big bag of potato chips, and a container of dip. Later on, for the first time, while they sat in Billy's parked car at the drive-in movie—*The Accidental Tourist* was playing and not *Rocky IV* at all—Laura put her arms around Billy and her tongue in his mouth.

His lips were salty and his breath tasted of beer. It wasn't even quite dark yet. While William Hurt's voice narrated the story on the screen, Billy ran his hands along the sides of her body. Laura moaned and felt electricity prickle beneath her skin. She couldn't remember ever feeling this way with Joseph.

With a trembling hand, she pushed Billy toward the driver's side of the car. He fell back as easily as a rag doll. "You're right," he said. "I don't want us to go too fast either."

The movie was almost over. They watched the ending in silence, having no idea what the beginning or middle had been. "I'd like to go home now," Laura said when the screen went dark. Billy returned the voice box to its stand and turned on the ignition.

After they'd left Palermo and were streaming along in the dark, sea-scented night, they began to talk. Billy said, "You seem better than when I first saw you this summer. I don't know . . . you're less jumpy or something."

"I am better." Billy's long thighs, clad in worn-out denim, appealed to Laura. She rested her hand on one. "In New

York, everything was so confusing. The phone was always ringing when my mother was sick. Her friends called every minute, wanting to know how she was. And later on, after she died, they still called. They couldn't stop talking about her, saying how sorry they were and what a unique person she'd been. . . .

"The house is so quiet now. I love never having to hear the phone. Or at least if it rings, it's really for me." Was she explaining anything? Would Billy think she was selfish? They were crossing a causeway from the mainland and an empty pickup rattled past them.

When the road was quiet again, Billy put his hand over Laura's. "If you want the truth, my mother thinks the whole setup over at your house is crazy. She says your parents never gave enough thought to you and Heather, but at least when your mother was alive, someone was around during the week. Now she says it's like both of them have abandoned you."

Laura did not answer at first. She needed to absorb the blow of his words, the way they suddenly turned things around and blamed her parents. She wondered what else Mrs. Ruzzo might have said.

They were almost home now, driving through Margate. At each traffic light they sat on their own side of the car, separate yet still connected. "What's your opinion?" Laura asked Billy.

"You mean about your parents?"

She nodded.

"I always liked your mother. She was always nice to me. She seemed too beautiful to be a mother, though." Billy put both his hands on the steering wheel, a serious driver, neither foolhardy or casual.

"And my father?"

"The first couple of summers you were here I never saw him. I didn't even think you had a father. Finally Gabrielle and I snuck through the hedge so that she could show him to me. He was out on the porch reading a newspaper. But he must have heard us giggling because he came over and yelled at us and chased us away. Boy, he scared me!"

They were turning onto Marion Avenue. Billy stopped at the curb and leaned across Laura to open her door. "I'm going to go home now. That way we'll both stay out of trouble."

"Thank you." Laura kissed him on the mouth. "You make everything so easy," she said.

That weekend, a few hours after her father arrived, Billy's story came back to Laura. She could easily imagine her father's voice, raised in irritation at being interrupted by two unknown little children. Weren't his own two children bad enough?

When he'd called Ventnor to say he was coming, she'd plucked her eyebrows in preparation for his visit. On Friday she hadn't gone into Atlantic City at all but spent the afternoon cleaning the house and ironing clothes to wear. Her father hadn't seemed to notice her at first, but at six when he was settled on the back porch with a beer and a cigar and the news on television, he said, "You're looking awfully pretty today. Have you gained some weight?"

Why bother telling him anything else? Laura thought. "About five or six pounds," she said.

"Good. You were too skinny before." Her father leaned back in the glider and ran his hand over the top of his crew cut. "You know what we haven't done in a long time?"

"What?" asked Laura dutifully.

"Gone to synagogue. Don't services start at eight-thirty here? You better call them and see."

In the kitchen, with the cord from the wall phone stretched full length, Laura got a recording: "Shalom, congregants. You have reached Temple Beth El. Our June 30th sabbath service begins at eight P.M. Rabbi Weinstock officiating for the vacationing Rabbi Dolgin."

The last time Laura had been in synagogue was at Union Temple in Brooklyn the week after her mother died. Her father had insisted they all go; he'd wanted to hear the rabbi say the *kaddish*, the prayer for the dead. As the man's deep voice chanted the ancient Hebrew words, Laura had almost fainted. It was as though he was calling to her mother across time and space, calling her back to them.

She dreaded hearing the *kaddish* again. But the rabbi at the Ventnor synagogue was a young man and he said it simply, in an ordinary tone. Everything about the place was simpler than the synagogue in Brooklyn. It was a big, square room with pine paneling and stained glass windows that were only two colors, yellow and red. The worshippers sat in metal folding chairs.

When the service ended, those on either side of Laura and her father turned to them and shook their hands. "*Gut*

111

Shabbos," they said, smiling. It meant "Happy Sabbath." Laura was glad she'd come.

It was dark outside and a soft rain had begun to fall. She took her father's arm, hoping he would not want to call a cab. She loved the smell of the wet sidewalks and the muted sounds of car tires and windshield wipers. But mainly she loved being the only one who was with her father, alone with him in the night.

"Why didn't you stand up for the *kaddish?*" he asked suddenly.

"I thought that was only if someone died in the last few weeks." Laura had stood up in the Union Temple and she'd seen her father stand during the prayer here, but she hadn't wanted people craning their necks and feeling sorry for her again and wondering who it was that had died.

Laura's father started walking fast; she almost had to run to keep up with him. They rushed down side streets where water dripped on their heads from trees; they crossed avenues against the lights. In a low voice her father said, "It's a sign of respect, that's all. Have you no respect?"

"You mean respect for Mommy?"

"And for me, too," said her father. "You and Heather, you have no idea what a marriage like that is. When your mother was dying, when I saw they couldn't save her, I wanted to die, too. Once in the hospital I got into bed with her and pressed against her under the sheets. 'Take me with you,' I said. But all she did was laugh at me, 'Get up, Danny. Don't be an ass.'"

Laura knew cancer wasn't contagious, yet the terrible sequence of the illness passed through her mind: her father's

112

neck would swell and then he'd begin to lose weight and then they'd have to hospitalize him. Didn't he love them at all? How could he even think of taking such a risk when she and Heather would be orphans? Laura stood in shock with the rain falling on her, as if this second death had actually happened.

But ahead of her, Laura's father kept walking, signalling with his arm for her to follow. She started running. It was pouring now. Laura's clothes were drenched and her wet hair slapped at her face as she ran. Her father was waiting for her at the corner, but just as she got there, the sole of one sandal buckled and she fell to the sidewalk.

"Take it easy. What's your hurry?" her father said, but Laura had already fallen. Under a streetlight, she could see that one of her knees was bleeding in a long dark stream. Her father handed her his handkerchief without comment.

She took off both sandals and held them by the straps. They were almost home, just two streets away. "I've been dating Billy Ruzzo," she said.

"Who is Billy Ruzzo?"

"Gabrielle's brother."

"Oh. And what does Gabrielle think about this?" Laura was looking at her father and she thought she saw him smile.

"Gabrielle doesn't know. It's a secret."

"Watch out for secrets. They can be dangerous," her father said mildly.

Laura and not her father had the house keys. She leaned toward the door, trying to find them in her purse, miserable because she was keeping him waiting.

"Let me do that," he said. Laura handed him her purse

and he immediately found the keys and opened the door. Inside the hallway, he turned on the lights. The glow of the electricity on the waxed floor made everything seem safe and civilized.

"What's to eat? I'm starved." Laura's father had taken his blazer off and was already moving toward the kitchen.

Unexpectedly Gabrielle came for a visit on Sunday morning. Laura had gone to a deli for lox and bagels and she and her father were eating breakfast at the white, wrought-iron table on the porch. It was a beautiful sunny day.

Laura was facing the garden when suddenly she saw Gabrielle standing on the lawn. She was wearing shorts and a halter top. "I came through the hedge," she said. "I hope you don't mind."

Laura's father pushed his chair back and went to the porch door to let Gabrielle in. "Quite the contrary! Laura and I were getting tired of each other's company. Last night she made me take her to a floor show at one of the casino hotels, but it was cancelled and all they had was mud wrestling. Mud wrestling! So we came home and were stuck with each other again."

"My brother Billy told me about that. It was at Trump Plaza, right? He said they had a whole different crowd in the casino last night. Some really weird people . . ."

"Do you want anything to eat?" asked Laura. She wished Gabrielle hadn't come, but she knew better than to let her father see that.

Gabrielle glanced at the slices of lox lying on waxed paper. "Thanks, but I already had breakfast."

"Bring your friend some coffee then, Laura." Her father pulled out a chair for Gabrielle. "You'll have coffee at least, I hope."

Gabrielle nodded, avoiding his eyes. She'd always been a little shy around Laura's parents.

In the kitchen Laura poured the rest of the coffee and turned off the coffeemaker; she wanted to hurry so that Gabrielle and her father wouldn't be left alone. But as she came back outside, her father was saying, "So your brother Billy's a blackjack dealer. . . . How old would he be now?"

"He's twenty-one."

"Laura tells me Billy's an interesting young man," Laura's father said.

"She does?" said Gabrielle.

Laura sat down at the table, her heart beating hard. "I never told you that."

"Well, not in so many words," her father said. "But still . . ."

Desperately Laura tried to imagine what her mother would have done to distract her father in the same situation. She turned to him and said, "Aren't you going to ask Gabrielle anything about herself? It's she and not Billy who's come to visit us, after all."

"True." Her father spread cream cheese on a piece of bagel and ate it in one bite. "I was getting to that. But first I wanted to tell Gabrielle she's growing up to be quite a beauty."

"Oh, Mr. Samuels," protested Gabrielle.

He raised his hand to cut her off. "Don't argue with me. I'm a middle-aged man and I know what I'm talking about."

115

"Well, then I guess I should say thank you." But Laura noticed that Gabrielle had crossed her arms in an effort to hide her breasts in the skimpy halter. "Don't do that," Laura wanted to say. "That only makes it worse."

Sadness and regret about Gabrielle washed over her. Their friendship seemed a million summer days away, in another universe entirely. She remembered the two of them on the beach, building the same kind of drip sand castle day after day in the belief that if they just once got it right, waves couldn't destroy it.

At least she could keep her father from baiting Gabrielle. Laura started clearing the table. "Tell my father about your job, Gabrielle. Then I want to show you something in my room. . . ."

"What was it you wanted me to see?" Gabrielle asked later when they were upstairs.

"That was just an excuse. Really I wanted to ask about what's been going on between you and Greg, but I didn't want to say anything in front of my father. You two are still going out, aren't you?"

"God, yes. We're together all the time, whenever we're not working. He just bought a new truck, a brand new Nissan, and some nights I don't get home until three or four in the morning. My mother just about has a fit." But Gabrielle looked happy when she said this.

"Could I meet Greg sometime? I'm not sure if I remember him from last summer . . . who he even is."

"That would be great! I've been wanting to ask you, but . . . we really haven't seen each other that much lately."

"Right," said Laura. She opened her bureau drawers and her closet, looking for her bathing suit. "Do you want to come swimming with me, Gabrielle? I didn't go yesterday because of my father so now I really want to."

"You know me, I'm not a very good swimmer. Besides, I have to get ready for work." Gabrielle followed Laura down the stairs and without saying why, they walked to the front door so they wouldn't have to see Laura's father. "Were you serious about wanting to meet Greg? You want to go out with us tonight?"

"What's tonight?"

"Sunday."

"I can't," Laura said. "I don't know when my father's leaving."

"Well . . . tomorrow?"

"Tomorrow's the only other night that isn't good for me."

She had the door open for Gabrielle and the bright noon sun flashed in. Laura wanted to go swimming. She imagined her body moving swiftly through the water, her pale green private world.

Gabrielle asked in a tense way, "How about Tuesday? It's my day off so we could pick you up earlier."

"Tuesday would be perfect."

CHAPTER
11

Sunday and Monday nights were reserved for Ari. The time they spent together was the high point of Laura's week—everything else led up to that. Ari was so sophisticated, a grown up, yet he seemed willing to accept her. Their routine never varied. Blackjack at Billy's table, dinner at Ivana's, blackjack again until two or three in the morning. Each evening he gave Laura five black chips to play with; she tended to win more often than she lost.

On weekday afternoons Laura still gambled in different casinos, at the five-dollar tables, but now it meant no more to her than practice. Playing cards should be second nature, she'd decided, like breathing. She shouldn't have to count the cards in her hand; she should read them at a glance. She shouldn't have to guess to bet; she should know the odds from the way the aces and high cards came up in the shoe.

Laura's motive for all this effort was simple: the better she played blackjack, the more she'd be able to impress Ari with her composure and skill. But every time she walked into a casino, she was scared. What would she do if they asked for her I.D.?

Ten days after Heather had taken her wallet back, it finally happened. Laura had been playing in Atlantis of all places, a casino known for being lowlife and down on its luck. Here the red carpets were stained and the dealers tended to be slow and clumsy. She was up about fifty dollars and had decided to move to another table because she didn't like the way the dealer was looking at her, with his face stern, as if he was angry every time she won. The table was full and when he started talking to the pit boss, Laura didn't think anything about it. But suddenly a security guard on the floor put his hand on her arm.

"This way," he said. "We want to talk to you." He was a skinny young black man. His badge identified him as Winston, but his uniform was so baggy it looked like it belonged to someone else.

"Take your hands off me." Laura made her voice low enough so that only he would hear. "What about my chips? I won them, they're mine."

"The dealer will give them to you. Don't worry about that." He was leading her to a door that said SECURITY. "They're going to card you. You got any I.D. showing your age?"

"No." Laura looked over at him, at the way he walked,

heels down first and his shoulders bouncing, like another version of the cool black kids she admired in New York. She made a quick decision. "I lost mine. You know where I could get another one?"

He paused. The door in front of them was closed but there was a glass window in it. "They'll make you leave your chips," he said. "You'll lose all your money."

"That doesn't matter." Laura felt giddy with fear and suspense. Had he even heard her?

Winston, the guard, put his hand on the door handle and turned his body so that Laura was hidden by his back. She was very close to him suddenly and could smell his freshly ironed clothes and the sweet oily pefume of his hair tonic.

"I have a friend, Benny. . . . he has one of them rolling chairs over by Indiana, near Claridge's. Say I told you to check him."

"Benny?"

Winston nodded and opened the door. "Come here," said a man in his fifties, sitting at a desk. Laura walked over to him. She'd left all her own identification at home so it was really only the casino's word against hers, but still they made her leave. Another guard took her out through the lobby. Winston had disappeared; she was sorry she didn't have a chance to thank him.

Outside on the boardwalk Laura walked directly to Indiana Avenue. The rolling chairs were a famous Atlantic City attraction. They were white wicker chairs on wheels, with canvas awnings to protect customers from the sun. A friend of Heather's had driven one last summer; he paid

$35 a day to rent it but she didn't know if he'd made money or not.

Laura had expected Benny to be black, but he looked Jewish to her. He said, "Yeah, sure . . . Winston. Now what did you say you needed?"

It was an overcast afternoon and the boardwalk was not very crowded. Laura legs suddenly felt weak. "Do you mind if I sit in your chair?"

"Be my guest." He wheeled it so it faced the beach. A row of sea gulls lined up on the boardwalk railing didn't even move.

"Can you get me an I.D.?" Laura asked.

Benny shrugged slightly and held out his hands, palms out. The implication was he could get her anything in the world, no problem.

"I want it to say that I'm Heather Samuels." She took a pen out of her pocketbook. "Here's the date of birth."

Each morning when Laura finished swimming, her mind was a blank, like a clean slate or an empty table or an egg. Her limbs were heavy and she could almost feel her ball joints rotating as she walked back to Marion Avenue across the sand. Usually at this time of day, at seven in the morning, there was no one on the beach. A jogger or two maybe, dressed in nylon running shorts and sneakers, but no one else.

That's why Laura was so amazed to see a big woman in a bright pink bathrobe blocking her way as she reached Marion Avenue. Laura was scared even before she recognized her. It was Mrs. Ruzzo.

"Laura, finally! This time I really won't take no for an answer. Come and have breakfast with me, no one else is up." Mrs. Ruzzo took Laura's arm and patted her other hand. "How brown you are! It must be from all that swimming. How long have you been down here now?"

"Four weeks, I guess."

"Time flies," said Mrs. Ruzzo. They walked up her driveway and in the back door.

"I'm sorry," said Laura, feeling her wet bathing suit. "I don't have a towel."

"That's all right. It's nothing to worry about. Nothing." Mrs. Ruzzo took a newspaper from beneath the sink and laid it on one of the kitchen chairs. "Sit down. Don't worry. I'll make both of us some coffee."

The last time Laura had been in this kitchen was the day she'd met Billy again. It seemed much closer than four weeks ago. *Billy.* He was like his mother in the way he took care of her, Laura thought, but he was gentler about it. Two nights ago when they'd last gone out, he'd told her a really sad story about a friend of his in the merchant marines who'd died of leukemia, a kind of cancer in which the person's white blood cells multiply out of control. Before Billy started working, he'd traveled all the way to Indiana to see his friend once more.

Mrs. Ruzzo brought coffee, orange juice, and a box of crullers to the table. Faintly, from upstairs, Laura heard a toilet flush. She hoped it wasn't Billy.

"So. I was sorry not to see more of Heather when she was here. She looked radiant, like a bride. But you . . . what about you? How's your summer going? Gabrielle says

122

you swim every day." Mrs. Ruzzo smoothed the lapels of her bathrobe and gazed at Laura expectantly.

"Almost every morning. Not when it's raining or like, not last Saturday because my father was here."

"But you've already been swimming and it's only seven-thirty now. What do you do the rest of the time?"

Laura's mind was empty and she felt panicky. Usually so quick to lie, she found she had nothing to say. She sat across the table from Mrs. Ruzzo while the refrigerator or the kitchen clock hummed and time stretched out ominously between them.

"I know about the evenings. I know you've been seeing my son Billy, but what do you do all day long?"

"You know about Billy?" Laura repeated. Gooseflesh rose on her arms. In her wet bathing suit, she was suddenly ice cold.

"That's a mother's job. A mother should know everything. I won't say a word to Billy, but let me give you some advice . . ." Mrs. Ruzzo leaned closer, clasping her coffee cup. "You're the one who stands to lose in this, the girl and not the boy. I'm not happy about Gabrielle going out night after night with Greg Wilkins either, but I brought her up to respect herself. You—I don't know what your mother brought you up to do."

Laura picked up her glass of orange juice. She had a sudden desire to toss it at Mrs. Ruzzo. She wouldn't do it violently, but gently and fast, with just a flick of her wrist.

"You look upset," Mrs. Ruzzo said. "Don't be. I'm sorry to criticize your mother. I don't like to speak ill of the dead." She was silent for a moment and then she put her hand on

123

her heart. "My concern is for you. It's you I worry about . . . such a lovely young girl with her whole life ahead of her."

"But I'm fine. Billy and I are just friends. We talk and he's really understanding and nice to me."

Mrs. Ruzzo nodded as if she already knew that answer. "But you have so much time on your hands, living alone in that big house with your mother's things everywhere you turn. I know you haven't seen me, but I've passed you in my car and I've seen you on the corner in broad daylight, wearing makeup and dressed just like she used to be —even down to that necklace around your neck. The first time I saw you, my heart stopped. I thought you *were* her."

Laura was still freezing, she felt like she could die from the cold. She reached across the table for her coffee but when she took a sip, her teeth clattered against the china cup.

"That coffee's cold by now, let me get you a fresh cup." Mrs. Ruzzo poured more coffee. "I know you're not going anywhere with Billy dressed like that because it's the afternoon when I've seen you and Billy's already at work. So tell me—where are you going? Is there maybe another man who admires you in high heels and jewelry and blouses so low your breasts stick out?"

"Stop spying on me," said Laura desperately. "Leave me alone."

Mrs. Ruzzo shook her head, but in a sad way, not as if she meant to argue. "That's just the trouble. Everyone's left you alone for years. Your parents—"

"They have not," Laura said. She stood up to leave, but just then she heard footsteps on the stairs, and Billy and his father came into the room. They were both wearing dungarees and seemed only half-awake. Billy smiled at Laura. His chest was bare. She did not want to look at it, but her eyes kept returning to the muscles along his ribs.

"Why, Laura Samuels . . ." That was Mr. Ruzzo, a funny, shy man who fixed boats for a living and never worked during the winter months. Laura had always liked him.

"Hello, Mr. Ruzzo. I haven't seen you all summer."

"I've been here," he said. "Lying low." He winked at her and went to open the refrigerator.

"Put on a shirt, Billy," said his mother.

"I really have to go," said Laura. She picked up the newspaper on the kitchen chair, wet with the impression of her body. "Where do you want me to put this?"

"Don't worry. I'll take it." And Mrs. Ruzzo crumpled the newspaper and held it in her hand until Laura was gone.

"What did your mother say about me?" Laura asked Billy. He'd come over to Laura's straight from work. She'd been expecting him and had already taken off her makeup and changed into old clothes when she met him at the door.

"Nothing . . . except she was glad to see you. My car's parked around the corner. Come on, let's get out of here." It was raining and instead of taking Laura onto the street, he led her through some bushes to the neighbors' yard on the other side. "It's a shortcut. Bert Danziger's a friend of mine. They won't mind."

The air was full of the sound of rain and of waves crashing in the ocean. Laura thought they'd go far away, but Billy only drove ten blocks. As he parked the car, he said, "I hope this is okay. I need to move around tonight."

They were at a miniature golf arcade where they used to play as children. It had concrete pillars and a roof, but it was open on the sides. Gusts of rain kept wetting them as Billy played through the eighteen holes.

"You look cold. Here, take my shirt." Billy handed her the flannel shirt he was wearing over his sweatshirt. The light in the arcade was dim and green, from the fake grass carpeting, or perhaps from the storm outside.

To Laura the whole evening had an air of unreality. They were the only people except for the attendant, who was enclosed in a small wooden booth. The arcade catered to children, and many of the holes involved painted plaster cartoon characters—Daffy Duck and Pluto and a clown like Ronald McDonald. In the dimness the white of those faces gleamed, whereas she could hardly see Billy standing next to her.

"How was work today? You never say anything about it."

Billy rested the short golf club against his pant leg and looked at Laura. "I don't want to encourage your casino fantasies," he said. "I know you still have them."

"I don't. Why should I? That time I went into the casino, it was only to see you."

"You never told me that. From what you said when we were sailing, I thought you went there just for the hell of it, because you're wild or something."

"Well, now that I know you like me, I can tell the truth. We were going out that night anyway, but I couldn't wait.

126

All that makeup and stuff—that was just so they'd let me in." Laura tried to remember back to the first time she'd gone to Trump's. Really, in the beginning it *was* because of Billy. Billy had given her the idea.

Right now he reached for Laura and gently pulled her toward him. He ran his two hands along the sides of her arms and traced the outline of each finger. Laura lifted her chin to see him better. His face looked serious, as dark and clouded as the sky. "I think I'm falling in love with you," he whispered.

Laura was frightened. "No, don't do that. I'm too young. . . . I'm not the right person."

"Nothing will happen. You trust me, don't you?"

She nodded and turned away, unwilling to let Billy see her. An echo of Mrs. Ruzzo's words suddenly came to her: "My heart stopped . . . I thought you were your mother." It was an old terror of Laura's that when she was grown up and not paying attention, she'd turn into her mother *and never even know it.* She swayed against Billy and held him tight.

"I'm finished anyway. Do you want to leave?"

"Oh, yes," said Laura.

But later on, after they'd driven to the beach parking lot at Longport and kissed each other until Laura's breasts ached and her face smarted from Billy's beard, she asked him, "Do I remind you of anyone?"

"Like who? I can hardly see you." A streetlight at the edge of the macadam was shining through the car window, but their breaths had fogged the glass.

Laura swiveled the rearview mirror toward herself and ran her finger across it. "You don't think I look like my mother?"

"No. She was a completely different type."

"Good," said Laura.

Billy moved over to the driver's seat. "I'm starved. Let's go to Dave's Diner. They have good fried fish dinners." He rolled down his window, then reached across Laura and rolled hers down, too. The ocean was so quiet they could hear each wave come in. The rain had finally stopped.

CHAPTER
12

Usually when Laura came to the blackjack table at Trump's, Ari would stop playing to greet her. But this time when she called his name, he did not even turn around. He was watching the cards come at him, shaking his head as they hit the table. Laura sat down. He looked tired, she thought. He'd taken off his jacket and loosened his tie. The sleeves of his white cotton shirt were rolled to his elbows. "Is everything okay?" she whispered.

"Not particularly. I've been losing all day."

Laura felt her stomach contract. Ari believed she was lucky for him; that was why he took her to dinner and gave her chips to gamble with and treated her like a worldly, grown-up woman. But what would happen if he lost?

Now the shoe was empty and Ari really seemed to see

her for the first time. "I'm glad you're here. Maybe you'll change the cards."

Instinctively Laura reached for her mother's necklace.

"No—hold on to the table. Please."

The dealer had been shuffling the cards and now he had them arranged on their sides in a line, ready to go back into the shoe. He handed Ari the yellow cut card, and Ari in turn handed it to Laura.

She eyed the cards fearfully, and then plunged the cut card midway through the line, thus determining which cards would come to Ari. The dealer cut the deck, lifting the cards in front of the cut card to the back of the line—now they'd be dealt last. Laura realized she'd been holding her breath. So much depended on this!

Ari handed her five black chips and rearranged his own chips on the table. Laura tried to count them without appearing to. He seemed to have at least thirty black chips, and the five he'd given her. She felt reassured—at least he wasn't completely broke.

Sunday night at the casino was usually quiet, but before the first hand had even been dealt, four Asian men sat down. They were middle-aged men in business suits who didn't speak any English. Laura thought they must be Japanese because Ari had told her once that the Japanese were serious gamblers. They each took five thousand dollars in chips and began betting. The gestures of blackjack were like sign language, she realized, a language without words, available to everyone.

She was so worried about Ari's cards that she failed to pay attention to her own, and once when she had twelve and the dealer had a five showing, she forgot she was supposed to stand. When she took another card, the Japanese men broke into loud protest. It seemed unfair to Laura that they could say whatever they wanted, insult her however they wanted, and she could not understand them.

"Why don't they mind their own business?" she complained to Ari. "Just because they can put five thousand dollars on the table, they must think they run this game."

He threw her a look of warning. "The mistake was yours. If I were you, I'd concentrate on my cards. And sometimes, you know, people born in other countries understand more than you realize."

"Is true," said one of the Asian men.

Heat suffused Laura's face. She took a sip of Ari's Scotch, but it tasted like steel in her mouth. She told him, "I don't want to play anymore. I think I'll just watch."

For more than an hour, no one left the table. It didn't seem to matter to the Asian men if they won or lost—each time one of them ran out of chips, he would pull another thousand dollars from his wallet. Their supply of money seemed endless. "Serious gamblers," Ari had said, but the whole time they played, they talked and joked as if it were a private party. Whenever the waitress came, they ordered gin.

The cards that night were terrible. In three shoes the dealer never broke, and each time that Ari had a nineteen or twenty in his hand with hundreds of dollars riding on it, the dealer seemed to pull twenty-one.

Finally it was close to midnight and Ari had only nine black chips left. The other men had left some time earlier.

131

"Do you want to move to another table?" Laura asked. She lowered her head so that her hair curtained her face. "Or do you want me to leave?"

"What did you say?"

"I can leave if you think your cards would be better with me gone."

Ari leaned back and rubbed his eyes. Then he did something that astonished Laura—he put his hand on her thigh. She was wearing her silk skirt and she was glad that the fabric was so thin and smooth for him to feel. It was the first time he'd ever touched her in a sexual way.

"We never had dinner. You must be starving," he said, pocketing his chips. Laura thought they'd go to Ivana's, but instead Ari led her into a large open restaurant behind the hotel lobby. The menus were huge and Laura was glad to hide behind hers, trying to gauge what it all meant—Ari's losing, his hand on her thigh, this break in routine.

He seemed distracted and ordered only a sandwich. While they were eating, he kept looking over her shoulder as if he were waiting for someone else. Finally Laura turned around, but no one was there, only the wide empty hallway leading back to the casino.

"Shall we?" he asked. And he signed his name to the check the waiter brought him. Laura wished she had the courage to suggest a walk on the beach or even that they go to another casino, but all she could do was to stay wordlessly at his side as they sat down once more at the blackjack table.

Ari lost nine hundred dollars in only two hands. He bet two chips on the first hand and then he bet the other seven and lost them, too. Laura had never seen him act recklessly. Her heart began to hurt. So there really was such a thing as a heartache, she thought.

"Bets please, sir," the dealer said. "Are you in the game or not?"

"I have no cash. I'd like a $3000 marker."

The pit boss came then and leaned across the table to show a paper to Ari. "Mr. Hassan, I'm sorry. I'm afraid you're at your limit. We can advance you only another thousand."

"Am I to thank you? You've already taken fifteen thousand from me today. Give me the thousand." Ari reached into his vest pocket for his own pen and signed his name on the paper. "Are you ready, Heather? Let's go."

Laura slid off her seat and followed Ari across the casino floor. Looking at his back, at the rumpled fabric of his suit jacket and the place on his neck where the dark hair grew to a point, she felt like bursting into tears.

"Pick a table you like. A five-dollar table would be fine."

Out here on the floor, it was much busier than in the baccarat section where Ari always gambled. People were screaming at a craps table, cheering and clapping because when a player threw the dice, everyone who bet on his numbers won. Laura didn't understand craps. It was nothing like blackjack, where every player was isolated, playing alone against the house.

The five-dollar tables were full, but finally two people left one and Laura and Ari sat down. She was relieved because this was chance; she hadn't chosen anything.

Ari started out with five-dollar bets and he started win-

133

ning. He upped his bets to ten and then to twenty and was still winning. To fifty and won still. When he had doubled his money, he put his hand over Laura's on the edge of the table. "I knew you could turn it around for me," he said. And her heart hurt more than ever.

The night wore on. Laura didn't dare go even though Ari had stopped paying attention to her. His face was glazed with a fine oil or perspiration and the shadow of a beard was on his jaw. He had begun to lose again. When the pit boss announced the last shoe, he pushed his towers of red five-dollar chips and green twenty-five-dollar chips toward the center of the table. "Give me hundreds for these," he said.

The dealer handed back eleven black chips. Laura was relieved. Now they'd leave and cash them in and walk outside on the boardwalk. She was sure a walk would soothe Ari. But he did not move from the table.

She took his wrist, seeing the tangle of black hairs and the heavy gold watch and the time three-fifty on it. "You can come back tomorrow and play. Stop now," she pleaded.

He didn't answer or move. He merely put his black chips out and waited. The bets had closed and the dealer had a ten showing. Two gray-haired women and Ari were left in the game. The dealer turned over the dark card and it was an ace. "Blackjack," he said indifferently.

Ari bowed his head for a moment. "Well, that's it, then. Let's go."

The boardwalk in the early morning light was still in Laura's mind but Ari instead took her to the bank of elevators in the lobby. Their brass doors shone, reflecting Laura and

Ari together. She was surprised to see how tall he was, a full head taller than she. "Would you like to come to my room?" he asked when the elevator doors opened.

There was not enough time to think of an answer. And why else, Laura asked herself, was she with this man when the cards themselves had come to seem flat and two-dimensional to her, without any real power.

Music was playing, drifting softly from the elevator walls. It took Laura a while to recognize the tune because it was so disguised by violins, but at last she placed Bruce Springsteen's "Tunnel of Love." She was humming it as she followed Ari down the hotel corridor. They were on the twenty-third floor. She hadn't been so high up since she'd left New York.

He had no room key, just an electronic card that he inserted into a slot on the door. A little green light flashed on the lock and he turned the doorknob. "Please come in," he said in a formal way, standing aside so that Laura could enter.

If she had had to imagine what a room in a casino hotel would look like, she would have imagined this room. It was dark green and the walls were covered with fabric. Heavy drapes hid the windows; the furniture was painted with a shiny maroon lacquer paint. The bed was enormous. Someone had turned back the covers and left two foil-wrapped chocolates on the pillow cases. Laura felt saliva come into her mouth. "Could I have one of those?" she asked Ari.

"Please. You must take both." He handed them to her and patted the bed beside him.

Laura sat down, taking the foil off the chocolates and

waiting to see what would happen. She felt both curious and helpless, as if she were ensnared in a dream.

Ari watched her as she ate the candy; his eyes were on her mouth. He said, "Why don't you open the drapes and then I can turn off this light."

Laura crossed the room and found the drape pull. It was a metal assembly and the drapes opened with the sound of ball bearings, smooth and oily. She looked out the window self-consciously, aware of Ari behind her. For a moment she had trouble placing the view—the roof of a building with vents and pipes, a slice of boardwalk, then a larger slice of beach and ocean. The window must be set at an angle, she realized.

When she turned around, Ari was lying on the bed with his hands folded behind his head. "Take off your sweater," he told Laura. "And your bra. Please."

It never occurred to her to refuse. She was wearing her mother's black cardigan and she let it drop to the floor. The push-up bra she'd bought with Gabrielle opened in the front and she took that off, too. She turned to face Ari, waiting for him to come to her. "Very nice," he said. "And now your skirt and panties."

Laura slipped them off. She had no stockings on, only her flat sandals and the necklace around her neck.

"Now cup your breasts in your hands and turn toward the window. Perhaps some lucky man on the beach will look up and imagine he has gone to heaven."

"What?" She'd heard him, but the words flew past her, making no sense.

"Why shouldn't we give pleasure to those below? Still,

if you'd rather not. I know—go over and sit on the bureau. If you face the bureau mirror, we can both see you."

When Laura had taken off her clothes, she'd expected Ari to undress, too, to touch her or caress her and to make her feel it was all right that she was there. But he had not moved from the bed and his voice was cool.

The lacquer bureau where she was perched had rounded edges and her thighs spread out on it with a sucking sound. She noticed that the paint in one place was blistered, as if someone had spilled nail polish remover on it. She was starting to feel afraid, but she didn't know what to do.

"There's a brush in the top drawer. Why don't you brush your hair? Such pretty hair . . . so dark and shiny."

"Don't you like me at all?" Laura asked. She wanted to sound sultry, teasing, but her voice, even to her, was a girl's voice, with a note of alarm in it.

"Have I upset you? I didn't mean to," said Ari, turning and sitting on the edge of the bed. "It's just that to-night . . . I'm sorry, but I can't bring myself to touch you."

Laura was flooded with shame. She remembered a time when she was eight or nine years old and going with her parents to a Broadway show called *Cats*. She'd gotten dressed up in her favorite dress, white lace with a yellow satin sash. But when she'd come into the living room her mother had started laughing. "That dress hasn't fit you in years and it's silly and monstrous. Take it off this instant. You'd look better naked."

But now she really was naked, alone in a hotel room with a man she hardly knew and the cold morning light coming in. Ari approached her across the carpet. He was still completely dressed and his feet in their shiny loafers and smooth black socks seemed to be moving in slow motion. Step by step, he came at her, and when he finally put his hands on her shoulders, she began to weep—whether in fear or relief, she could not have said.

"Heather, Heather . . ." He led her to a closet near the entrance of the room and took out a white terrycloth bathrobe for her. "Are you cold? Put this on."

Quickly and neatly Ari stripped to his shorts, hanging up each piece of clothing as he took it off. Even his socks went over a hanger, Laura saw, and he had plastic shoe trees for his shoes. He put his watch on the bureau and plumped the pillows on the bed. "Come to bed now. It's almost five."

Laura had been wanting Ari to take her in his arms, but now all she felt was a churning nausea. If only she could leave! She looked around. The door to the room had a chain across it and the window was a set pane of glass cemented into the wall. "I'd better go to the bathroom," she said.

She turned on the bathroom light and ran the water in the shower to drown her sobs. Sweat covered her body, and she remembered the first weeks after her mother's death, when she'd lain under the covers in her hot, closed bedroom, unable to get out of bed. In the mirror her face seemed unfamiliar, garish with makeup, the mascara running in streams from her eyes.

"Are you all right?" Ari knocked lightly on the door.

"I'm fine. I'm just taking a shower," Laura answered. Then she stepped into the water.

She took a long time in the bathroom and when she came

out, Ari had drawn the drapes again and was in bed. She thought he was asleep but the moment she lay down, he curved his body to hers. Black hair covered his body and the contrast in their skins was startling and fascinating. He said, "Promise me you won't cry anymore."

"I won't cry," Laura said. She closed her eyes. All the feeling had drained out of her and she wanted only to sleep.

CHAPTER
13

In her dreams Laura was in danger, but she believed that if she could only arrange her body properly in the bed, she would be saved. She turned and thrashed, looking for the right position, but she kept coming up against a soft, un-yielding barrier. Not until Ari put his hand on her shoulder and shook her, did she realized it was him. "Bad dreams? Time to wake up," he said.

He watched from the bed as she stood before the bureau mirror, dressing and putting on her makeup. "Last night you looked like a child sleeping with your washed face and your damp hair on the pillow. Do you know, even your eyelashes were damp?"

Laura was worried he was going to ask how old she was

then, but he disappeared into the bathroom and she heard the shower run. In fact Ari had never seemed curious about her at all. In Ivana's while they were having dinner, he'd talked to her about gambling, or about politics and world events. He seemed to know every news story in detail. "I need to," he'd told her. "It affects my work."

The clock on the night table said eight-fifty. Laura turned on the television, watching a talk show with the volume turned off. She could hardly see the picture because sunlight from the window was falling across the screen, but it didn't matter. As soon as Ari got out of the shower, Laura planned to tell him she was leaving. She'd say she'd meet him tonight in the casino and then never show up.

Under her flimsy silk clothing, which looked so wrong and dumb now that it was daylight, Laura's body felt bruised all over. Her mind hurt, too, with the effort of trying to shield herself from Ari's treatment of her a few hours ago in this room. She longed to go back a few weeks—to ride her bike along the boardwalk as it was getting dark, to neck with Billy in his car again, to swim through the cold clear ocean to the Ventnor Pier and past it.

But when Ari came out of the bathroom and asked her to have breakfast with him, Laura agreed. After all, they wouldn't be alone together, and it seemed easier than saying no. The skin on Ari's face was shining from the razor and he was dressed differently than she'd ever seen him, in chino pants, new tennis shoes, and a white knit shirt with a collar. As they waited for the elevator, she cast about for something to say—a small neutral remark she could make.

Above the buttons on the elevator there was a keyhole Laura had not noticed. Into it Ari fitted a metal key. "What's that for?" she asked.

"Oh, it's a silly thing. A club they have for people who spend a lot of money in the casino."

The elevator rose through the floors but no one else got on. Laura said, "Is it all right for you still to go there?"

"What do you mean?"

"Well . . . because they stopped your playing."

The elevator doors opened. Ari blocked them with one hand and held Laura back with the other. "It's nice of you to be concerned, but you have no idea what you're talking about. You don't know the arrangements I have with the casino."

"Oh," said Laura in a small voice. Ari was making her feel intimidated.

"Wait! Is this elevator going up or down?" asked a man who was in the hallway with a briefcase and a tennis racquet.

"Up," said Ari, stepping out. He ushered Laura to one of the doors along the corridor and opened it with the same metal key. Inside, floor-to-ceiling windows faced directly into the sky. Laura blinked in surprise. The tables in the room were set with linen tablecloths, and waiters in tuxedos glided among them, but there was only one other customer—a woman dressed in a white satin bathrobe who sat motionless with a cup of coffee in her hand.

"Are the raspberries fresh this morning?" asked Ari.

"Flown in from New England a few hours ago," the waiter assured him as he led them to a table.

"Very good. I'll have cornflakes with raspberries. And juice and coffee."

"Me, too," said Laura.

Ari nodded toward a table under a crystal chandelier. "Look on the buffet table. You might see something else you like." The room was decorated in a strange way, Laura thought, as she walked across it. Besides the dining tables, there were leather couches and a television with an enormous curved screen. Murals of a rural countryside were painted on the walls but there was also a polished dark wood statue of Buddha.

On the serving table, croissants and Danish pastries were piled in silver bowls. Laura almost gagged with the thought of so much richness. "Nothing pleases you, Heather?" whispered a voice behind her. Laura knew it was Ari, but she had forgotten for the moment that she was Heather and did not answer.

"Didn't you hear me calling you?" he asked. She had almost bumped into him when she turned around.

"I guess I was thinking of something else."

Ari nodded, looking at her with the corners of his mouth turned down.

Who is he to judge me? Laura thought suddenly. *He's only a gambler; I don't have to be afraid of him.* She picked up her pocketbook and walked to the door. The sunlight flooding the room propelled her and so did her fatigue, which was so great that nothing seemed to matter much anymore. "Good-bye. I'm leaving now," she told Ari.

He took her arm firmly. "What do you mean? Stay and

eat your breakfast. They just brought our fruit and cereal."

"I'm not hungry."

"But I need to talk to you. I have something to say."

A waiter was watching them from across the room. A memory of her own body, naked and submissive, came to Laura.

"I want to apologize for last night." Ari's fingers around her arm loosened. "Please," he said. "Don't make me have to beg. . . ."

Reluctantly Laura returned to their table and sat down. Or rather she felt herself sitting, her knees bending, her thighs lowering onto the chair.

"You're very beautiful. I'm sure you must know that. The first time I saw you . . . how long ago? I don't remember, but it was in the afternoon. I wondered why they would let someone so young into the casino. You had on a black dress, made of cotton, I think, and your arms were sunburned."

Laura wanted to protest, to lie again, but Ari held up both palms toward her. "Your age doesn't matter to me. Eighteen, nineteen, it doesn't matter. I wanted you from the first time, but I was winning. You understand . . . I couldn't stop playing because I was winning."

"But last night when you lost, you didn't touch me anyway." Laura couldn't look at Ari now and instead poured milk into her cereal. The raspberries in the bowl floated to the top, gleaming dark red in the milk.

"I miscalculated; I allowed myself to lose too much and my desire left me. It happens that way sometimes. But tonight, you'll see, I'll play better. Only small bets this

144

time." Ari smiled at Laura and handed her the sugar for her coffee as if everything between them were settled.

"But where will you get the money?"

"I only need a couple of hundred to start with. I have at least that much back in the room. Pocket change."

The room was air-conditioned, almost cold, but Laura noticed wet stains of perspiration under Ari's arms. *He's the one who's afraid,* she thought. *He's scared he won't be able to stop losing.* "I have to go," she said. "Really. They'll be wondering at home where I am."

Ari stood up with his napkin still in his hand. "You'll be all right if I don't take you down?"

"Sure."

"Then I'll see you in the casino tonight. Around ten? We'll have dinner at Ivana's. A sepcial meal, to celebrate . . ."

"Yes," said Laura, knowing it was a lie because she'd never see Ari again. *Let it be the last lie,* she told herself.

She walked down the corridor and pushed the elevator button. Suddenly she couldn't wait to get outside! She'd take the bus home and wash the makeup off her face and go swimming. Maybe she'd call up Gabrielle. Maybe she'd even go visit her father and Heather in New York for a few days—a break from being alone in Ventnor sounded good right now.

The elevator stopped at almost every floor, but Laura didn't mind. She felt happy and exhilarated, as if she'd escaped a terrible fate. People seemed to be checking out of the hotel, whole families with suitcases and children. They smiled at Laura and she smiled back.

145

But at the bottom, in Trump Plaza's pink marble lobby, Billy Ruzzo was standing. He was dressed for work in his metallic vest and string tie and when he saw Laura, he said her name like a question, just that one word: *Laura*. Then his face went very white and his arm straightened and hit her across the chest, knocking her to the floor.

The marble was cold and Laura lay crouched on her forearms with her ears ringing and her skirt hitched up to her thighs. Some people who were waiting for the elevators moved forward to help her. But Billy was already there, kneeling at her side. "You bitch," he whispered. "You were lying to me all along."

Laura wanted to talk to him, to explain that she was through going to the casinos. Blackjack, fancy clothes, makeup, false names—it had all been a mistake. She wanted to tell Billy that, but no words came to her.

As she lay on the floor, she saw a security guard pass among the people who had gathered, a crowd of them now. He grabbed Billy's elbow and yanked him up. "What happened here?" he yelled, giving Billy a push with his hand. "What do you mean hitting a guest?"

Billy didn't answer. The security guard kept his grip on him and spoke to Laura. "I hope you're all right, Miss. I'll send someone over to help you. Trump Plaza deeply regrets this incident." It seemed to Laura that the guard had made a mistake. She was the one who shouldn't be here, the one who had no right. But instead he was leading Billy away. They turned a corner and were gone.

A big man with a coarse, lined face and gray hair showing from under a cowboy hat helped Laura to her feet. "Can you get up, honey?" he drawled in a Southern accent. "He hit you pretty hard."

Laura nodded, still too stunned to speak. She held her arm and rotated her left elbow until pain stopped it at a forty-five-degree angle. She thought she must have used it to break her fall or landed on it somehow.

"Are you staying in the hotel? Can we take you up to your room?" he asked. He had a woman with him and they both stood waiting for Laura to make up her mind.

"No. Thanks anyway. I live near here, I can take the bus home."

"Bus! Nothing doing. We're going to get you a cab." He put his arm around Laura's shoulders to support her. And the woman moved to the other side of Laura and took her hand. She was a small, dark-haired woman wearing bright red lipstick and a tight sheath dress. A mink stole hung over one shoulder. "Did you know him? The one who hit you, I mean?"

Laura cradled her sore elbow. "Yes. He was my boyfriend . . . used to be my boyfriend, I guess."

"Just like my first husband," the dark-haired woman said companionably. "He used to hit me all the time. Just like that, too . . . in public places. He didn't care."

The man didn't join in the conversation. Maybe he didn't hear them talking, or perhaps he knew the story already.

They were moving slowly across the lobby. The clerks at the front desk looked up past the customers they were waiting on and began whispering to each other. A doorman hurried to start the revolving door moving, but the man escorting Laura shook his head. Then he and the woman walked

Laura through a swinging door so they wouldn't have to let go of her.

They led her to a covered, cobblestoned area outside the lobby where doormen and bellboys greeted new guests and parked their cars and helped them with their bags. While Laura watched, a white limousine pulled up, discharging three couples in evening clothes. The license plate said Quebec, so perhaps they'd come from Canada and had been driving all night.

After conferring with the man, the doorman put a silver whistle to his mouth and called for a cab. Immediately, as if it had materialized just for this occasion, a car pulled up. It was from a neighborhood car service, not a real cab at all, but an old battered Buick with a light on top. The driver smelled of cigarettes and when Laura was settled inside, she smelled their dank odor in the cab's upholstery, too.

Through the open backseat window, the man slipped a fifty-dollar bill into her hand. "This should get you home okay."

"I can't take this," said Laura, amazed.

"Ah, don't worry, honey," the woman told her, pulling the man away and squeezing Laura's arm. "It's not real money. He won it last night at roulette."

"Thank you for helping me," said Laura. But it was too late, the cab was already pulling away. She turned around and saw the couple, arm and arm, waving good-bye to her. Sometimes people could be so kind, it was shocking.

The driver lit a cigarette. "Where to, Miss?"

"Ventnor. Marion and Pacific," said Laura. She sat in a

148

corner of the backseat, watching the familiar streets of Atlantic City flash by. Iowa, Brighton, Morris, Chelsea. When she got home, she'd go swimming and take a nap, and then when night came, she'd go next door to see Billy.

Her stomach turned as if she were face to face with him right now. She saw his angry eyes and heard him say "You bitch," again. How could he say that if he really loved her? Laura leaned out the window and let the hot summer wind blow in her face, filling her eyes with dust and tears.

They pulled up at the corner of Marion Avenue. The driver braked suddenly and turned around. "That'll be seven dollars."

The fifty-dollar bill the man had given her outside Trump's was still crumpled in Laura's palm. She flattened it and handed it to the driver. He looked at it and shook his head. "I can't change this."

"Then keep it." Laura walked down Marion Avenue without a backward glance. She did not want the driver to thank her. She remembered what the woman at Trump's had said: It wasn't real money anyway.

She let herself into the house and went right up to her room, opening all the windows and pulling the shades. Without even looking in the mirror or washing her face, she changed into her bathing suit. The house was hot, still and silent. A faint smell of perfume hung in the air.

Laura had forgotten her rubber flip-flops and the tar pavement outside on Marion Avenue made her feet burn. But the sand on the beach was even worse. She knew from experience that the best way was to keep moving. Weaving among the beach umbrellas and blankets, among sunbathers and picnickers and children playing, she finally reached the cool wet sand at the ocean's edge.

With a feeling of relief, like coming home, Laura threw herself into the waves. They were high today and pounded her chest as she swam crosswise through them. When she was out far enough, past the people bobbing and bodysurfing where the long breakers came in, she began swimming the crawl parallel to shore.

Her left elbow hurt each time she lifted it above her head, but the pain was almost welcome to Laura. It made her believe that Billy would have to forgive her for being in Trump's this morning. After all, he was the one who'd hit her—he had hurt her, too.

When she came out of the water, she sat down on a deserted beach chair with a picnic cooler and a thermos next to it. Maybe she'd start bringing picnics to the beach now that she wouldn't be gambling in the afternoons anymore.

For the first time since school had ended, Laura thought about her schoolwork. She could ask her father to bring down her Spanish book. She'd almost failed Spanish and had gotten out of summer school only by promising to review her whole junior year and take the final over again in September. He teachers had known about her mother's death and so they hadn't expected much, but the truth was that Laura hadn't done any work in school all year.

Idly her hand went to her throat, her fingers feeling for her mother's heart necklace. But she touched only warm salty skin. She lifted herself out of the beach chair and looked beneath it. But the necklace wasn't there. How long had it even been missing?

Last night in the casino, she'd run the heart along its chain more than once for luck, and she thought she remembered doing that in Ari's hotel room, too. Between the bathroom door and the bed had been a low table, like a night table. Laura closed her eyes. On its red lacquer surface lay the necklace—just where she'd put it before getting into bed with Ari.

As she walked home, Laura kept her hand at the base of her throat. Everyone she passed seemed to be staring at her. She had thought she never wanted to see Ari again, but now that her mother's necklace was lost, she felt as if she had nothing left to protect her or keep her safe in the world.

CHAPTER
14

"Carol? It's Laura Samuels. Is my father there?"

"Sure he is, honey. I'll put you through right away."

There was a hum and Laura heard her father's voice, a little too loud so that she had to hold the phone away from her ear. "Laura, it's lucky you got me! I just came back from lunch and I have a meeting later with a supplier out of the office. Things are really crazy here but it's good to hear your voice. To what do I owe the honor of this call?"

Sitting in her bathing suit on the screened porch, with the phone cord pulled around the corner from the kitchen, Laura said, "I miss you, Daddy," and tried not to cry.

"Well, of course, I miss you, too. You know I wanted to come down over the weekend. And if it hadn't been for the damn slowdown at the plant, I would have been there, too. I told you that on Friday."

"I know," said Laura.

"Are you lonely? Heather keeps telling me it's wrong to let you stay down there when you have to be alone so much of the time."

"Give Heather a message for me. . . . tell her to mind her own business."

There was a pause and a rustling sound, as if her father were rearranging papers on his desk. "I wish you girls could get along better. Your mother hated it that you fought. 'They should be best friends,' she'd say. 'There's nothing like a sister.' Of course she and your Aunt Mimi were always so close. And your Aunt Joan, too. But I'm probably not telling you anything you don't already know."

"That's okay," Laura murmured.

"Aside from missing me, is there anything I can do for you? You have the credit cards and the checkbook if you need money."

"I don't need any money. But, Daddy . . . something bad happened." Laura looked down and saw that she'd tracked sand across the flagstone floor of the porch. That meant it was everywhere, sprinkled in a line from the front door through every downstairs room.

"Are you going to make me guess what's wrong or are you going to tell me?" There was a note of impatience in her father's voice. She was running out of time; he was probably worried he was going to be late to his meeting.

"You know Mommy's heart necklace . . . the one you gave her for Valentine's Day when we were little?"

153

"Of course. What about it?"

"I was wearing it and I lost it."

"Jesus, Laura! That wasn't costume jewelry! I paid a lot of money for that necklace. Plus the sentimental value. I told your mother years ago that she should sell it, or at least trade it in for something else. But she wouldn't because she said it symbolized our love. Who gave you permission to wear that necklace? Did I say you could?"

Laura couldn't answer; it was a trick question anyway. She pulled on the telephone cord and wound it around her wrist until the coils were stretched almost flat.

"Can you retrace your steps? Where do you think you lost it?"

"If I knew that, it wouldn't be lost."

"Don't be sarcastic, young lady. This is your fault and I expect you to do everything in your power to find that necklace. Actually I was planning to give it to your sister as a wedding present . . ."

"Oh, great."

"Let's not fight," her father said. "I have a lot on my mind." There was a brief, accusing silence. "How about if I call you tonight to see if the necklace has turned up?"

"Okay." Laura stood up so quickly that the glider hit the porch wall. "Are you coming next weekend?"

"It depends what happens at the plant this week. If I don't have to go to North Carolina again, of course I'll come." He paused. "You think we don't care about you, Laura, but you're so wrong. Your sister and Leo and I had dinner together last week and we spent the entire meal talking about you. Heather's very concerned. Do me a favor? Give her a call, just to let her know how you are."

"Okay."

"Promise?"

"I promise."

"That's my girl," her father said. "I'll speak to you to-night."

Laura hung up and went to find Heather's new number. Not that she had anything to say to her sister or wanted to talk to her, but she was worried that her father might check to see if she'd called.

Heather and Leo were already living together in Leo's apartment in Brooklyn Heights. Laura could imagine the place perfectly, remembering Leo's admiration of her grand-parents' china and their etchings from the 1940s. It would be a floor-through apartment in an old brownstone, perfectly furnished, with shiny windows and floors.

She imagined their phone ringing on a delicate, dark mahogany end table. It rang four times, then Heather's voice came on with a hum and a click. "Hello, this is Heather. Leo and I aren't here right now. But if you'll leave your name and number, we'll get back to you shortly. Have a lovely day."

For a few seconds, before the beep that signaled to begin the message, Laura considered disguising her voice and saying, "Eat shit." But of course she didn't do that.

"Hi, Heather. This is Laura. I just spoke to Daddy and he told me to call you so I'm calling you but you're not there. I'll speak to you later. 'Bye."

She'd planned to nap, and she did sleep for a while. But late in the afternoon when she woke up, hot and disoriented, every sound on the street alarmed her. She could hear cars passing and children playing. Rock and roll music came faintly through the air. She imagined it was playing on Billy's radio, propped on the windowsill of his bedroom.

She knew that usually he'd still be at work until six, but Laura was so convinced it was Billy's music—it was just the kind of old rock and roll he liked—that she threw off the covers and stood before the window, her hands flat against the screen. She wanted to see Billy and get their confrontation over with. She couldn't wait another minute!

With shaky fingers she brushed her hair and opened her bureau drawers to find something to put on. But when she looked at her clothes folded on the shelf paper her mother had once lined the drawers with, they had no meaning or associations for her. She couldn't choose what to wear. If Heather were there, she could have asked her and she even felt tempted to call her sister back in New York and leave that message on the machine: *What should I wear, Heather? Tell me what to do now.*

Blindly she stuck her hand into the bottom drawer and pulled out a T-shirt and some faded black dungarees. It was much too hot for dungarees but Laura put them on anyway.

She locked the house and walked through the hedge and up the Ruzzos' driveway. Pausing outside their kitchen door, she heard the murmur of voices through the screen. Someone laughed and then the voices rose, though she still couldn't make out any words. Probably they were having an early supper together.

Last summer and for all the summers Laura could remember, she'd eaten with the Ruzzos two or three times a week. The whole family usually ate at the kitchen table. Those meals were fun with everyone crammed close together and eating piles of food without ceremony, just reaching for things, not having to wait or say, "Please pass the butter," the way they did at Laura's house.

By the time she'd come home, at eight or eight-thirty after it had gotten dark, her own family would just be sitting down to dinner. "No, thank you, I'm not hungry," Laura would say as she walked into the cool shadowy dining room. "Did you eat at the Ruzzos again?" her mother would ask. "No, I'm just not hungry," Laura would say, lying automatically.

She put her knuckles out and knocked on the wooden part of the Ruzzos' screen door. It rattled in its frame a few times and she heard Mrs. Ruzzo say, "Come in." Slowly Laura pushed the door open. She had no real plan or idea what to do. But in her mind she saw the kitchen table with its blue-and-white-checked cloth and an empty chair and a place set for her between Billy and his mother.

But there was no place set, no empty chair. There was only a silence that seemed to leap in judgment on Laura the moment she walked in the door. As she crossed the kitchen floor, no one moved aside to make room for her and Billy didn't go to the dining room to bring an extra chair. Instead the whole family sat like statues, looking down at their plates of chicken and mashed potatoes, lifting their glasses of milk to their mouths.

Finally Mrs. Ruzzo said, "You have some nerve to come here. Haven't you done enough damage to Billy?"

"Mom—" Billy put his hand on his mother's arm.

"No, let me talk." Mrs. Ruzzo lifted her elbow out of his grasp. "I kept my mouth shut twice before when I saw her dressed like a hooker, and look what happened."

"Mom, this is between me and Laura."

"You're my son and I don't want to see you hurt. I don't think there's anything wrong with that."

"Listen to your mother, Billy," said Mr. Ruzzo in a low voice.

Laura wanted to leave. She wanted to turn around and walk out of the Ruzzos' kitchen forever, but first she had to make Billy look at her. If he'd meet her eyes, even for a moment, they could be together again. "I'm sorry, Billy," she said.

Mrs. Ruzzo half-rose in her chair. "You're sorry? You're sorry? Well, maybe that's a first for you so we should all be grateful."

"Listen, Ma—" put in Gabrielle.

"What is it, Gabrielle? This has nothing to do with you."

"But, Ma, nothing so terrible even happened. Billy's going to get his job back."

"What do you mean?" Laura asked.

Gabrielle started clearing the plates, passing back and forth in front of Laura. "He was suspended because of what happened in Trump's this morning, but on Friday the case comes before a board that oversees casino workers. Like a

158

labor board. They're not too strict, though, because they need workers. They don't have enough people to do the jobs as it is."

"Maybe I can help," said Laura. "I could go to the meeting and tell them it was my fault."

"Don't do us any favors. You've done enough," Mrs. Ruzzo said.

Laura's face smarted and she felt the woman's words like slaps. Mrs. Ruzzo pretended to be so nice but underneath she was a bully and no one in her family ever tried to stop her. Laura said, "Why are you being so mean to me? I think you must be doing it on purpose."

"Mean? I'm the last one who's mean! All those meals you ate here, all the times you stayed overnight, sleeping in Gabrielle's room, coming down to breakfast in the morning. But did your mother ever have Gabrielle over to spend the night? Would she even sit down with me and have a cup of coffee? 'Thank you but I'm too busy now,' she'd say. 'Some other time perhaps.'

"I couldn't believe she got cancer. And don't think I didn't cry when she died. Any mother dies, it's a terrible blow for the children. So that's why I never said anything to Billy, either that you were seeing him or doing something worse in your makeup and your mother's clothes. You were disturbed, anyone could see that. But it's no excuse to hurt someone or to get them fired from their job."

"I haven't been fired, Mom. Suspended isn't fired." At last, from across the table, Billy looked at Laura. She smiled at him and he raised his hand to his hair in a strange little salute. Her gaze held his for what seemed like a long time.

"I'd better be going," said Laura. No one protested or said good-bye. Mrs. Ruzzo began to serve the dessert, ice cream with chocolate sauce, putting a glass dish before each person.

Outside it looked like a thunderstorm was coming. The leaves on the hydrangea bushes hung limp and motionless, and the sky had a strange green cast. Despite everything, Laura wished she could go back to the Ruzzos' kitchen again and throw herself on their mercy. "I didn't mean it. I didn't know what I was doing. Please forgive me. Please, please, please," she'd sob, kicking her heels on the linoleum floor.

But Laura was too proud to do that. Instead she let herself into her empty, locked house and cried, the way she usually did, alone. She walked up the stairs crying, then she took her pillow in her arms and lay on a rug underneath the windows, drawing her knees to her chest and crying until sobs shook her body, breaking over her like waves.

Rain came in through the open windows and lightning flashed, outlining objects in the room with perfect clarity. This made Laura realize it had grown dark. Hours had passed. The phone on the bedside table was silent; her father had never called. But what difference did it make? She was almost an adult now, wasn't she? She could take care of herself.

Laura turned on a light and walked to her bureau mirror. Her cheeks were swollen and streaked with tears and her hair was stiff from saltwater. She liked the way she looked, though. She reminded herself of some bag ladies she'd seen in New York, who wore fragments of cast-off clothing but still had a kind of style.

There was one person left who wanted to see her, one person who thought she was important. Ari. He was at Trump's waiting for her now and he had her mother's necklace. It was already nine-thirty. If she didn't hurry she was going to be late.

Laura went to the kitchen to fix herself a snack, and then she began walking to Atlantic City. She had no money with her and she was wearing no makeup or disguise of any kind. But when she came to the red open wall of the casino at Trump's, the security guard posted there didn't even glance at her. He seemed oblivious to her faded dungarees, her tangled hair, her T-shirt. She *was* like the bag ladies, Laura thought triumphantly; no one wanted to bother her.

She held herself erect and crossed the casino floor. This time, instead of focusing on the rich people with their gaudy jewelry and fancy clothing, she noticed the others—the black people and poor people who clung to the edges of the casino, playing the slot machines, or those who stood behind the players at the tables, watching the action, sometimes stepping in, but only for a hand or two.

Her steps quickened as she came to the baccarat section of the casino, to the table where Ari played. A woman dealer who she recognized was there, and three men in suits were seated on stools. Laura came around to the side, waiting to smile at Ari. But the men were strangers, and she thought she saw shock registering on their faces.

Laura turned and left. She didn't want any of the players signalling for the pit boss to look her over. She knew instinctively that if Ari wasn't at that table, he wasn't in the casino at Trump's, and so there was no reason for her to stay, either.

She made her way to the hotel lobby and leaned on the registration desk, resting her cheek on her forearm, until one of the clerks came over and said, "Yes? Can I help you?"

"I want to call a guest. Is Ari Hassan in his room? It's on the twenty-third floor, but I don't remember the number."

The clerk turned away and punched something into a computer. "I'm sorry but we have no Ari Hassan listed."

"But he was here this morning. He stays here every Sunday and Monday night."

"Wait just a minute." The clerk was a beautiful young black woman, thin and glamorous, but Laura imagined that her eyes met Laura's in a sympathetic way.

She punched the keys of the computer again, tapping her fingers while she waited for writing to appear on the screen. "Yes, you're right. He was here. But he checked out at noon."

"What about next weekend? Did he make a reservation for Sunday night?"

"No, I'm sorry. We have nothing." The clerk smiled at Laura and the mask of her perfectly made-up face seemed to tremble. "Good luck," she said. "I hope you find him."

The boardwalk outside the hotel was lit with yellow halogen lights and the people strolling by looked burnished in their glow. Laura hadn't been on the boardwalk at night before and she was surprised by how safe it seemed. She walked all the way to the end of the casino strip until the

162

boardwalk abruptly ended in a ramp down to the beach. She'd taken off her sandals and her feet were stinging with splinters. Around her, the smell of the sea rose up, rich and mysterious.

On the way back, in one of the rows of honky-tonk storefronts that linked the casinos together, Laura noticed an open fortune-telling booth. There were several in Atlantic City; they were rumored to belong to gypsies. "The grandmothers steal little children," her father had warned her when at nine or ten she'd asked to have her fortune told.

But the old woman sitting outside the booth did not look like a thief. She was a fat woman and wore a housedress and sequined eyeglasses. A flowered scarf covered her hair. When she saw that Laura had stopped, she stood and beckoned to her.

Laura believed in psychic powers; she felt she needed all the help she could get. She read the horoscopes in the *Daily News* and when she wished on the evening star or on the candles of her birthday cakes, she kept her eyes squeezed shut, carefully wishing for other people's happiness as well as her own.

"Do you want a palm reading, or the crystal ball, or the tarot? Or I can do all three for only nine dollars." The fortune-teller led Laura through a blue plastic curtain like a shower curtain, and into a small, stuffy room. Inside a glass case were several strange objects, dried herbs, cards with pictures on them, a teacup, and a smudged crystal ball.

The woman lifted out the cards and the crystal ball, though Laura had still said nothing. "I can see you're in great need. Open your palm." Her touch was surprisingly gentle and her fingers were long and fine.

"I have no money with me but I can pay you tomorrow."

The fortune-teller sighed and shook her head. "Do you expect me to believe you'll come back? How many have ever come back? But you're a young girl still, a girl from a good family, I can see it in your hand."

Her fingertips brushed every part of Laura's palm and then she pressed the pads of Laura's fingers. For several moments she did not speak. Her eyelids closed and flickered as if she were dreaming. She sighed. "You will find something you have lost," she said. "It is valuable but it can only bring you sorrow. Leave it where it is.

"You have a good memory and you're fond of excitement. Your digestion will give you trouble when you're older. Avoid fried foods. Your lucky numbers are three, seven, and one. Soon you'll be going on a trip."

She opened the case again and replaced the crystal ball and the cards. "Come back tomorrow with my money. Nine dollars," she said. "Now we'll see if I was a fool or not."

"But all you did was the palm reading," objected Laura.

"Five dollars. It's my minimum price."

As Laura walked home along the boardwalk, she thought about her fortune. Something she had lost—that must be the necklace. She kept her eyes wide open, scanning the dark beach and the people going into the casinos. Three times she thought she saw Ari, a tall man carrying two leather suitcases, but each time it was someone else, and once it was even a woman.

164

CHAPTER
15

That week Laura swam more and rented movies, adventure stories and comedies, watching them sprawled on the king-size bed in her parents' dark bedroom. She was waiting for Sunday night. If Ari came back to Atlantic City on Sunday night, she knew that she could find him.

Every evening at ten the phone rang; it was either her father or sister calling. Laura talked to both of them the same way, assuring them that she was fine.

But they must not have believed her because at eight-thirty Friday morning while Laura was watching *Superman*, Heather and Leo walked into the bedroom. She hadn't heard them come upstairs. She was wearing lace shortie pajamas, and she immediately folded her legs under her so that the bottoms would not gape open in front of Leo.

"Daddy didn't mention you were coming."

Heather lay down next to Laura, fully dressed, with even her high-heeled sandals on. "Aren't you glad to see us?"

"Yes," said Laura. It was true. She was happy to have them there because now the weekend days would be easily filled up.

"It was late when we decided to come and we took the seven o'clock helicopter," Leo said. "We didn't call because we didn't want to wake you." He smiled at Laura and took Heather's hand. The sound of *Superman*, glass breaking and gunshots, went on in the background.

"Do you mind if I turn that thing off? It's making me nervous." Heather leaned across Laura and turned off the VCR. "Ah, much better. You shouldn't be inside, anyway. It's a beautiful day."

Leo raised the window shades several inches. Sunlight came into the room, falling in bands across the rug. "Do you play tennis, Laura?"

"I'll play if that's what you want to do. Is that what you want to do today, play tennis?"

"It's a good idea," said Heather. "But that's not why we came." She glanced at Leo. "We want to persuade you to come back to New York with us on Sunday. I don't know what's going on, why you called Daddy up crying, but all of us agree you've been here long enough."

"Did Daddy say I have to come back?"

"You know him. He's so preoccupied with everything . . . but when I said I thought you should come back, he said, 'fine.' Actually you might want to stay with us in Brooklyn. Leo's got a couch in his study and he's gone all

166

day long. You and I could do things together and you could have your friends over if you wanted."

"None of them are in the city now," said Laura.

"But I'd be there; at least you'd have me. Who have you even been seeing in Ventnor? Daddy mentioned something about Billy Ruzzo, that you were dating him. What happened? Didn't it work out?"

"We had a fight," said Laura. She got up from the bed. "Excuse me. I'm getting dressed. This is embarrassing to be in my pajamas."

In her room, Laura stood with her hand on the closet door and thought about leaving Ventnor. She pictured herself in New York, walking on the hot, steamy streets. But nobody could make her go, certainly not Heather. She needed Sunday night and maybe Monday night to find Ari. After that, she'd see.

A few blocks down the boardwalk were free public tennis courts. They were cement courts with cracked surfaces, but they were so close, Leo said, that it was silly to go elsewhere. As they walked from the front walk of their house onto Marion Avenue, Laura slipped between Leo and Heather. She held her racquet and a new can of balls tightly, laughing as if someone had made a joke. Laura hoped that Mrs. Ruzzo would be looking out her kitchen window so she'd see Laura with her own family to protect her.

They didn't actually play tennis, just rallied back and forth, Heather and Laura on one side against Leo. Laura enjoyed it. She liked the feeling of competition, the way the ball soared from her racquet sometimes, landing in the back court and making Leo run. He didn't seem to mind, though, and kept complimenting her on her swing. "Your father's right," he said. "You're a natural athlete. It's amazing."

"What about me?" asked Heather, pulling her ponytail tight and walking toward the net.

"You! I've always said you can beat me at any game."

After that, whenever Leo paid attention to Laura, even in a way that was only courteous, Laura was aware of Heather's eyes on them. It reminded her of how Heather had acted about Douglas Gold, her first high school boyfriend. He wasn't much, he was short and studious, and Laura had been only twelve at the time. But still, whenever Laura came into the living room and Douglas was there, Heather would run at her, flapping her hands. "Get out of here," she'd scream, "Stay in your room. I'm telling Mommy."

All Laura had wanted was to find out what was on television or to get some candy from the dish on the coffee table. She hadn't seen what Heather had been so worried about; she didn't see what Heather was so worried about now.

Late in the afternoon, they were all lying down, Laura in her room and Leo and Heather downstairs in the living room, when the telephone rang. "It's for you," Heather called up.

"Hello, Laura?"

It was Billy Ruzzo. His deep, blurry voice made Laura's heart drop. "Are you there? Who was that who answered the phone?"

"My sister."

168

"Oh, at first I thought it was you."

"A lot of people say we sound the same."

There was a silence and she could hear Billy breathing into the phone. "The hearing was today. I just wanted to let you know it went all right. I start work again tomorrow."

"That's great, Billy!"

"Yeah, I thought you'd be relieved."

Actually Laura hadn't even remembered about the hearing, so much had happened since.

"I miss you, Laura."

She put the phone on the pillow next to her and closed her eyes. "I miss you, too. I've been afraid even to walk by your house."

"What are you talking about?"

"Your mother . . . I think she hates me, and probably Gabrielle does, too."

Over the phone, Laura heard a door closing. "Listen, I can't talk about this now," said Billy. "Are you doing anything tonight?"

"I don't know. Heather's here with her boyfriend. Her fiancé, I mean. He's nice. You'd like him."

"But it's you I want to see."

"We don't have to stay with them," said Laura.

But two hours later when Billy showed up, Heather led him into the living room before Laura could even get to the door. She and Leo sat on the couch, on either side of Laura, and Billy looked around and then sat in one of the wing chairs.

His long frame seemed out of place in the delicate room,

and he shifted nervously, trying to get comfortable. Leo was dressed in slacks and a shirt with a collar, but all Billy had on were shorts, a net tank top, and sneakers without socks.

It was as if he were on trial. Leo was a lawyer and Heather was in law school, and they kept asking Billy questions— what had he been doing since high school, did he like the merchant marines, how did he like working in the casino. Laura was nervous, but Billy answered everything in a neutral, respectful way, using few words.

"What are you two planning to do tonight?" said Leo finally, getting to his feet.

Billy rubbed his palms on his thighs and looked at Laura. "I don't know. There's a big fair in Avalon, over in Cape May. I thought maybe we'd go there."

"I love fairs," said Leo. "When I was little, the rides scared me, but now I love them."

"They have some good ones at this fair, too. You could come if you want . . . you and Heather."

"Excuse us a minute," Laura pulled Billy outside into the back garden. "Why did you invite them?"

"Look, they're worried about you. I want them to trust me, that's all." He lifted her chin with one finger and smiled at her and winked. Tenderness had softened his face; he looked younger than she remembered, almost her own age.

The screen door slammed. From the patio Heather said, "We decided we would like to come . . . if it really is okay."

Laura was amazed at how well everyone got along that evening. She couldn't have imagined Leo and Billy would have anything in common, yet at the fairgrounds they stuck together, teasing Heather and Laura about being scared of the rides.

"No, we're not," said Heather. "Just because we don't want to break our necks on the roller coaster. . . ."

"In my opinion, that makes us smart, not cowards," said Laura. The two of them were standing behind Leo and Billy at one of the shooting games. They'd had chili dogs and french fries for dinner, but they hadn't gone on any rides yet.

Billy propped a rifle against his shoulder, squinted, and pulled the trigger. A duck on a conveyer belt of ducks fell backward with a tinny sound. He pulled the trigger four more times and two more ducks fell over.

"You're some shot!" cried Leo.

Billy collected a pink furry teddy bear for his prize. "Do you know what Laura's been doing all summer?"

"What do you mean?" asked Heather.

"Just that. Do you know where your sister's been every day when you were going about your business in New York? Does your father know?"

Laura put her hand on Billy's arm. "Please, Billy . . ."

"This is for you." He gave Laura the teddy bear. Its fur, which had looked so soft, pricked at her forearms. The four of them walked away from the beaten dirt and the lights of the shooting game to a darker place.

"Why are you doing this? Can't you stop now?" Laura whispered urgently to Billy.

But he shook his head and drew her to the ground, pulling her back against the V of his bent legs. Heather and Leo faced them, arranged in the same way. They were sitting on the grass between two lanes of concessions. In the distance a merry-go-round turned; its twinkling mirrors and hurdy-gurdy music made Laura want to cry.

"Tell us what you were going to say," said Leo.

"The last time I saw Laura was Monday morning. She was coming off the elevator at Trump Plaza wearing a black sweater and so much makeup you could write your name in it. She looked like a little whore." Behind Laura, Billy shifted uneasily. "I lost it. What I did to her was unforgivable—"

"Billy, don't! It was my fault. You don't have to say anything about that!"

Heather and Leo were leaning forward. Even in the washed-out darkness, Laura could see that they were shocked.

"I don't understand," said Heather. "What were you doing there, Laura?"

She shrugged, unable to decide how much to say. "Why don't you ask Billy?"

There was a silence and Billy sighed loudly. "She'd been with a man the night before in the casino, a blackjack player. Someone I know who's a dealer saw her with him. Later my mother told me she used to see her plenty of times during the day, too, all dressed up, on her way into A.C."

Leo said, "But I thought you had to be twenty-one to get into the casinos."

"All you need is someone else's I.D. or a fake one. The guards at the door usually won't bother you, and if they see that you have cash at the tables, lots of times the dealers won't bother you, either."

172

"That's what happened to my wallet," Heather said in a flat voice. "She stole it for my I.D."

Laura jumped to her feet. "*She? She?* I'm right here! You're talking about me like I don't exist."

"Take it easy. No one's ganging up on you." Leo stood up and helped Heather stand, too.

Heather said, "I kept wondering, I thought, what is there for Laura to do all day? I should have known. I should have figured it out."

"Why?" asked Leo. "None of this is your fault."

"But we've hardly come down all summer. God, Leo, she's only seventeen!"

"And you're only twenty-two, so why don't you take it easy? Stop trying to be her mother, for God's sake. You'd both be better off. Has anything so terrible even happened to Laura? Think about it. She's been sneaking into the casinos, so what? Billy saw her in the hotel in the morning, so what? Whatever he did to her, that's between them."

In Laura's fantasies Heather would have attacked her, screaming and sobbing, twisting her wrist in an Indian burn or pinning her to the ground. She would have made Laura feel guilty of committing every crime. But Heather only stared at her and didn't say a word.

"Don't worry, Heather. Leo's right. I'm fine."

"I can see going to a casino out of curiosity, to find out what it's like, like Leo and Daddy and I did at the beginning of the summer. But why keep going? Was it because of that blackjack player?"

"No."

"Well, what was it then? Are you addicted to gambling?"

173

"Of course not! Don't be stupid!" The two of them began walking ahead of the men, crossing the last stretch of darkness before the midway. She knew Heather was upset, but with each step she took, Laura felt lighter, as if her secrets were stones tossed to other people.

That's why she thanked Billy on the Ferris wheel. It was the first time at the fair they'd been alone. As soon as they were settled into their little car and the wheel started moving, picking up other passengers, she said, "I was mad at you at first when you were telling Heather and Leo about me going to the casinos."

"But they're your family. I couldn't stand it that my family knew and yours didn't. My mother's so defensive. All she wants to do is to shut you out to protect me, which is some joke, anyway."

"What do you mean?"

"I'm here, aren't I?" Billy put his hands over Laura's on their car's metal safety bar. "I can't stay away from you."

They were at the very top of the Ferris wheel now and suddenly it jerked forward and began turning fast.

"Don't worry, it's perfectly safe," said Billy. "Look around you. Enjoy the view."

Laura tried to. The Ferris wheel was rising again and the people and the stands and the pale green treetops seemed to fall away beneath them, twinkling with distance.

"I don't mind anymore."

Billy put his arm around her. "I knew you'd like it once you got used to it."

"No. I mean, I don't mind that you told Leo and Heather

I was going to the casinos. I'm glad you did. It's a relief not having to hide what I'm doing anymore."

"But you're going to stop, aren't you? That's the whole point. They'll make you stop."

Laura shrugged. "Maybe. They said they want to take me back to New York with them on Sunday."

"Good," said Billy. "I'll miss you but, good."

"Wait a minute. There are some people I need to say good-bye to first. Your sister, for example . . ."

And Ari, she thought. *I need to say good-bye to Ari and get my mother's necklace. Is that a crime?* She kissed Billy on the mouth and the car rocked hard in the sky.

CHAPTER
16

It wasn't that she wanted to go to the casinos. If Laura had had her choice, she would have looked for Ari anywhere else. On Sunday evening, when she was getting ready to go into Atlantic City, spreading the layers of makeup on her face, she felt faint and nauseous. The chalky sweet smells that came out of the bottles and tubes made her want to gag. And when she was done, the person who stared back at her in the mirror looked like a stupid clown.

She'd begun her preparations early, as soon as Leo and Heather left. They'd forced her to spend an hour with them in the living room after breakfast Sunday morning, going over her lies, her reasons for wanting to stay in Ventnor for two more days.

Finally they telephoned Danny Samuels to arbitrate. "Let

her stay," he said. "I can drive down Wednesday and pick her up. If she leaves with you, we'd have to bring her things later and close up the house. This way it saves a trip."

The three of them were waiting at the curb for the cab that would take Heather and Leo to the helicopter when Heather suddenly marched up the Ruzzos' driveway and rang their bell.

"What did you say to them?" asked Laura, outraged, when Heather came back.

"I saw Mr. Ruzzo," said Heather. "Billy wasn't there."

"And?"

"I told him to give Billy a message." A cab had turned onto Marion Avenue and was moving slowly, looking for their address. "I told him to tell Billy to keep an eye on you."

"Jesus, Heather! I can't believe you did that!"

"Don't you trust your sister?" asked Leo.

"I've known her longer than you have," Heather said. She threw her bag into the backseat and slid in after it. " 'Bye, Laura. We'll call you every night."

That didn't worry Laura. An hour later, just before she left for Atlantic City, she took the phone off the hook. Let Heather get a busy signal, let her keep calling until she figured it out. Laura knew Heather wouldn't want to come back to Ventnor in the middle of the week just because the phone was off the hook.

As she was walking along Pacific to the bus stop, an empty cab drove by. Impulsively Laura raised her right arm to stop it. She was in a hurry and it was rare to see cabs cruising around here. But as the cab drew up to the curb, she recognized the driver. He was the same one who'd brought her back to Ventnor the morning after she'd been with Ari, the morning Billy had hit her.

She was so rattled to see him that she walked toward the entrance of the nearest house as if she'd never meant a cab to stop at all. She stood on the people's porch, hoping they wouldn't think she was a burglar, and waited for him to leave.

The cab didn't move for what seemed like five minutes to Laura. Perhaps the driver had recognized her, too, and was expecting another fifty-dollar bill. But nobody came to the door and finally, slowly, he drove off.

Laura tried to tell herself it was a good sign. If she could find the same cabdriver twice and not even be looking, then certainly she'd find Ari. It was six in the evening but the sun was shining brightly. That might be a good sign, too.

When she came into Atlantic City, the boardwalk was like a party. One of the hotels had hired a brass band, and clowns were moving through the crowds, handing out balloons to children. Everywhere Laura looked, people seemed to be celebrating. She could hardly bear to go into the dark red holes of the casinos—that was how she thought of them now.

She'd decided to start with Trump's and look in the casinos on the right, then the ones on the left, closer to Ventnor. Laura didn't think Billy would be working now; he'd said he was on the first shift again.

She rushed around the casino floor, scanning every blackjack table. She was used to the setup—six or eight blackjack tables clustered together with the wheel of fortune, roulette wheels, and craps tables in between.

But even though she knew where to look, Laura still got mixed up. She saw four people in wheelchairs playing roulette together and realized she'd passed them several times before. She checked her watch; nearly an hour had gone by. She'd been walking in circles and hadn't even known it.

Before she left Trump's, she decided to stop at the bar for a drink. One of the lounge acts was performing, a trio with a girl singer, and Laura watched enviously. What would it be like to sing on stage, to work every night with people who really knew you and then be applauded by strangers?

"Can I buy you another drink?" a man asked. He was in his forties with a thick face and a small brush mustache. He sat down at Laura's table without asking and loosened his tie.

"No, thank you." She stared stonily ahead, hoping he would get the point and leave.

"Nice act. I like that girl singer. But you're much sexier than she is. I've been watching you." The man grinned, pulling his lips tight over his teeth. Laura looked down to avoid looking at his face, but what she saw was worse. His thighs in the chair were moving in and out, touching along their length and then opening again.

She hadn't paid for the second drink yet, but she jumped up from the table and ran from the casino, clutching her purse to her chest. When she was outside, in a world that

179

had now turned to night, Laura finally looked back. Of course the man was not there.

Sweat had broken out in her armpits and along her hairline and she felt shaken and dirty. Ari had never approached her in that way. He'd waited for a long time and then asked politely for her consent. She paused by the boardwalk railing to let the breeze from the ocean cool her, and then she went into the casino at Caesar's.

It was full of people and motion and color and noise, and Laura was easily lost in the crowd. She walked over to the first blackjack table she saw and looked down at the cards on its green felt surface, mentally playing the hand in front of her, trying to focus. But perhaps because she had no stake in the game, the cards made no sense to her.

She wandered through Caesar's as she had at Trump's, directionless, making circles and slow figure eights around the tables until she found herself outside again.

As the night wore on and she drifted from one casino to another, things began to repeat themselves ominously. The rooms and the decorations and the games looked the same, and the people too seemed to repeat and multiply.

She saw gamblers who looked like everyone she'd ever known—her parents' friends, the elevator man in her building in New York, the Korean couple who ran the grocery store on her corner, the attendant in the miniature golf arcade where Billy had played golf. And she imagined she saw the man from Trump's bar again and again, in every casino she went to, in every corner.

The only person Laura did not see, in all the hours that she searched, was Ari. She knew his dark and glowing face would have leaped out at her like a beacon. But now it was four in the morning and the casinos were closing.

Laura sat down on a low, semicircular stone wall facing the boardwalk on the seaside. Pillars held up a frieze of flying fish and sea horses and dolphins skimming waves. It was all that remained of Atlantic City's old convention hall, an archeological curiosity from an earlier time. Dawn showed at the horizon, but a few stars were still out, floating high in the sky.

In front of Laura was Atlantis, the casino where she'd been asked for I.D. and thrown out. There had been constant rumors and reports in the newspaper that it was bankrupt and corrupt, and that it would soon be closing, but nothing had happened yet. Atlantis was the first casino she'd been planning to go to when they opened again at ten.

She was getting ready to leave, to look for a cab home, when she saw Ari walk from the swinging doors of Atlantis. It was just as she'd imagined—his walk, his dark suit, the way he paused for a moment to get his bearings, putting his hand over his breast pocket to check his wallet.

"Wait," Laura said, half-rising from the stone wall. But the word came out as a whisper and Ari didn't turn around. He was walking fast, up the boardwalk away from her. Perhaps he was staying at Trump's after all. Laura began following him, keeping several yards behind. It had been a reflex but once she'd started, she continued.

At four the boardwalk had filled with people that the casinos had disgorged. For those who didn't have the money for rooms at the hotels, the beach and the boardwalk were the best and safest refuge. Benches along the boardwalk

181

railing were filled with old couples, and young people, too, sitting patiently with their purses and shopping bags and their plastic coin cups for the slot machines, waiting for the casinos to open again. These were the day-trippers and twenty-four-hour players who came one day and left the next without buying lodging and sometimes not even meals.

Ari never turned to look at them. He passed Trump's and kept going, walking fast. Laura followed him, almost running, keeping track of him by his white cuffs and the white slice of shirt collar above his jacket.

Just before they came to Showboat, the last casino, Ari stepped off the boardwalk onto a dark little side street. Run-down apartment buildings lined the block, and there was trash on the sidewalk. Laura's breath came shallowly. She could hear her feet in their leather-soled sandals striking the pavement, but Ari never turned around.

On a corner at Atlantic Avenue a squat two-story building with a neon sign that said CARIBBEAN MOTEL DRIVE-IN appeared. At its entrance were a series of vending machines and Ari dropped some coins into one of them. Laura was so close to him that she heard the can of soda land with a thunk at the bottom. He stood for a moment drinking it and then unlocked one of the downstairs rooms.

Laura crept closer when she saw the light go on behind the curtains. The number on the room's door was 7 and next to it was a webbed plastic deck chair as if the occupant might want to sit there and watch the sights all day. She was thinking about this, wondering what it would be like, when Ari opened the curtains from inside.

She could see him perfectly, but she thought that all he'd

182

see would be his own reflection on the dark window glass. His jacket and tie were off and he was unbuttoning his shirt. He ran his palm over his cheeks, feeling his beard, and then she realized he was using the window as a mirror.

Suddenly the light went off and Ari rapped on the window twice, hard. They were only a few feet apart. Had he known all along that he was being followed? She ducked and fled, trying to keep her body low. "You are such a stupid coward," she told herself. "What is the matter with you?"

She ran on Atlantic Avenue while the words echoed in her footsteps. She should never have followed Ari; she should have greeted him the moment he'd walked out of Atlantis, just taken his arm and said, "Hello, there, I've been looking for you."

That would have been so simple. They could have gone for coffee somewhere and talked to each other in a nice way. But now Laura was stuck. She'd have to come back to the Caribbean Motel again before the casinos opened. She could imagine what Ari would think when he saw her waiting outside the door of his room, but she'd ask him about her mother's necklace right away so he wouldn't get the wrong idea.

It was getting light now and the buses were running. Laura stepped onto the first one she saw. On the way home she stared out the window, seeing her own reflection over the pale and gritty streets of Atlantic City. At Marion Avenue she walked home and put her house key in the lock like an automaton.

She lay down on her bed but could not sleep. While Laura waited to go back to Ari, images of her mother went through her mind. When her mother got dressed, she'd put everything out on the bed in layers as if it were a person—handbag, jewelry, and dress on top; slip, underpants, and bra beneath them; and at the end of the bed, going down to the floor, stockings and shoes.

Her routine never varied; only the outfits varied. Suits for lunches with her friend at restaurants, skirts and cable-knit sweaters to play golf in, cocktail dresses at night. In the hospital she'd worn silk nightgowns with lace inserts that Laura and Heather had ordered for her from catalogues. They'd bring the catalogues into the hospital so she could choose.

As if she were counting sheep, Laura counted the clothes in her mother's wardrobe. The morning breeze circled over her through the open windows. Soon she was asleep.

She found the Caribbean Motel without any trouble, but now, in broad daylight, she could see the cement-block construction, painted pale green, and the scorched and littered grass in the courtyard. The neon sign had been turned off; no one was around. Laura had not eaten breakfast and as she rapped on the door of room 7 with her knuckles, she felt she might faint.

There was no answer. She rapped again and pulled at the doorknob. It was not even nine o'clock. Surely Ari wouldn't have left for the casinos yet. He couldn't disappear again. He had to be here. Laura walked to the window. The curtains were drawn but there was a crack in the middle where they didn't quite meet. Laura looked behind her quickly and then she pressed her face to the glass.

It took a moment for her eyes to focus because the light in the room was so dim. Then gradually she began to make out objects—the corner of a bed, a chair with clothes flung over it, a bureau. At first all she saw on the bed were rumpled sheets, but then they moved and Ari's head and arm appeared. Laura drew back guiltily; sleeping seemed too intimate an act to be watching without consent. She'd wait on the deck chair by the door until Ari woke up.

But suddenly her attention was caught by a glint of gold on the bureau. The sun must have come out from behind a cloud, come through the crack in the curtains, and hit it at that moment. It was Laura's mother's heart necklace, tangled in its chain.

Next to it on the night table were a pile of chips, a few bills, and some other jewelry, Ari's cuff links perhaps. And there was also a gun—a small black revolver. Its shape loomed up at Laura, imprinted on her brain from all the gangster and cop movies she'd ever seen. Yet there was something familiar about it too, like the DayGlo plastic water pistols they'd been allowed to have as children.

Laura moved back from the window slowly, step by step, until she tripped on a curb at the edge of the courtyard. Both her knees were skinned and bleeding but she hardly noticed. The dark blood was staining her silk skirt but she kept on walking backward.

She didn't think the gun had anything to do with her. It was a gun for gambling or for getting money to gamble with. But still, it was a weapon. Did Ari know where she lived? The first night they'd met, she'd told him her house was on Marion Avenue, but Marion Avenue was a long street and she was pretty sure she hadn't given him her address or even said it was near the beach.

Laura's thoughts spun out of control. The house in Ventnor looked so solid, but anyone could break in. She thought about the coal chute in the basement, the one she and Joseph had used to come into the house last winter. All they'd done was to lift the hatch and open the basement door, which didn't even have a lock. She thought about the dining room in back with its big windows reaching the ground, how hidden they were by the garden hedge, how easily they'd break, with just a tinkle of glass.

She didn't want to stay in the house alone—not for one more night. Maybe she could stay at Billy's. Then Laura remembered that he'd already be on his way to work. Gabrielle might be home but Laura really hadn't spoken to her in weeks. As for Mrs. Ruzzo—Mrs. Ruzzo probably wouldn't even let her in. She'd bar her kitchen door and yell at Laura and tell her to get herself out of her own mess.

"Are you all right?" a man on a motorcycle who had stopped for a red light was looking at Laura. "You got blood on your skirt. You want me to take you somewhere?" He was a black man in black leather clothing, and when he raised the plastic face shield on his helmet, she saw that his smile showed concern.

"Thanks a lot. Could you take me to Ventnor?"

He nodded and Laura sat down behind him. As they zoomed off she suddenly realized she'd left her pocketbook behind, on the curb in front of Ari's room.

186

CHAPTER
17

Every sound on the street terrified Laura. She had let herself in through the basement and wedged a chair under the doorknob of the basement door near the kitchen. She had put the chain lock on the front door and locked all the windows and drawn the curtains.

Now she was sitting in the living room, in the dead center of the house, waiting for every car to pass, for every set of footsteps to keep going. Laura had tried her father at work but he hadn't come in yet. His secretary had promised to give him the message that it was urgent.

In Laura's mind Ari's gun was in his pocket and he was already moving toward her. There was no address card in her wallet, no driver's license, but she had a charge card at the Ventnor Rite Way and if Ari found her purse, he could probably trick the store into telling him where she lived.

"Stop it. Stop imagining things," she cautioned herself, but it didn't work. When the phone rang, she shuddered and jumped, just as if she had been shot. She raced for the kitchen and picked up the receiver on the second ring.

"Is that you, Laura? What's this all about? Carol tells me it's important, yet all night last night the phone was off the hook. That's what the operator said."

"Daddy, can you come get me? I want to go home."

"Right. We already worked that out. I thought Heather told you. I'm coming on Wednesday."

"No. Right now."

"You mean today?"

Laura slid down the wall and sat on the kitchen floor. She nodded, which made no sense because her father could not see her. "Yes."

"But why? What's the hurry? All summer you want to stay there alone and now you don't want to stay for two more days."

Laura closed her eyes and saw the gun in Ari's pocket again. "Remember when I said I lost Mommy's necklace? Well, I didn't really lose it . . . I left it in a man's hotel room. And now he might know my address. I'm scared he's coming here."

"Does this have anything to do with the casinos? Is the man someone you met there?" Laura's father sounded outraged, as if he'd been personally insulted.

"Yes," she said, almost whispering.

"You never get it, do you, Laura? If the law says nobody

188

under twenty-one can go to casinos, didn't it ever occur to you there might be a damn good reason why?

"You're probably just exaggerating. . . . still, you better lock the doors. I should have listened to Heather in the first place and made you come back with them on Sunday, but all right, I'll drive down. Just wait there."

He muffled the receiver and shouted. "Carol, call my garage and tell them to have my car ready in an hour."

He was coming. Laura couldn't believe it. She'd asked her father to do something that was inconvenient and hard for him, and he'd actually said yes. She hadn't cried so far today but suddenly her eyes were brimming with tears.

"Can you pack and be ready by three? I'd like to get home fairly early."

"Okay. Thanks, Daddy."

"Don't thank me," he said. "I'm your father." And then he hung up.

Laura walked back into the living room and threw herself on the couch and sobbed. She cried until her throat ached and her cheeks stung from the salt in her tears. A pillow beneath her face had a dark wet place on it where she'd been crying. She turned it over and plumped the other pillows. Then she went upstairs to pack.

"Hello. Gabrielle?"

"No. Who is this, please?"

Laura caught her breath, resisting the impulse to hang up the phone. "It's Laura. Is Gabrielle there?"

There was a silence. Probably Mrs. Ruzzo was trying to

decide whether to lie or tell the truth. "She's just on her way to work. Don't talk to her long." Somewhere in the house, a radio went on.

"Laura! It's me." Gabrielle's voice dropped to a whisper. "Listen, I'm coming over. I really want to see you."

"Don't use the front door. Come through the hedge," Laura said.

She was surprised at how emotional she felt when she saw Gabrielle on the patio in her freshly ironed work uniform. She wasn't wearing sandals as she usually would, but laced shoes with thick rubber soles. Then it hit Laura that every day she'd been running back and forth to Atlantic City, Gabrielle had been standing on her feet in a hotel kitchen, preparing food.

Laura wished she could apologize for not being a better friend. She led Gabrielle into the kitchen and poured her a glass of milk and put out some chocolate chip cookies from a supermarket package. "I'm leaving today," she said.

Gabrielle nodded. "That makes sense. I probably would, too, if I were you."

"My father's coming in an hour. I called him this morning and asked him to pick me up."

"Does Billy know?"

Laura shook her head. "He thinks I'm going Wednesday. We were supposed to see each other tomorrow night. Could you give him a message? Could you tell him I had to go and that I'll call him from New York?"

"Sure," said Gabrielle. "He hasn't talked about you much. Billy's pretty secretive. But the other day he called me into his room and said you were going to be leaving soon. He said to remember that you were the one who was a stranger here and that you needed our help."

Gabrielle was holding her milk glass and she looked at Laura over the rim. "The only thing was . . . you didn't seem to want to see me. Like, for example, you never met Greg that time you said you would. We kept calling you to find out where you were, but the line was busy. Greg's the major person in my life right now. . . . I might end up married to him."

"I know. I'm sorry, Gabrielle. I think I was a little crazy this summer." Tears filled Laura's eyes and she brushed them away impatiently. Why had she started crying again? She didn't want Gabrielle to feel pity for her.

"Don't apologize. It's not really your fault."

"Yes, it is," said Laura.

The doorbell rang. Laura stood up and reached for the edge of the table with both hands. Her skin tingled as if all the blood underneath it had drained away.

"Aren't you going to answer the door?" asked Gabrielle.

"Will you get it? Don't open it, just look out the side window and come and tell me what the person looks like. There's someone I don't want to see."

"Okay." Gabrielle put her milk glass into the sink and walked toward the front of the house, the skirt of her uniform bouncing against her legs.

The doorbell rang again. Then, as Laura stood in the kitchen, half-hidden behind the refrigerator, she heard the front door slowly open. What was Gabrielle doing? She heard her talking and then a man's low voice. Footsteps came toward her.

"He told me he was Heather's fiancé, so I figured he was okay," said Gabrielle.

The man said, "I gave her no choice. I told her if she didn't let me in, I had a key."

Leo Kramer was standing beside Gabrielle in the kitchen, a briefcase in one hand and his suit jacket in the other. He looked hot and worried, as if he'd rushed for a long time to get there.

"Your father asked me to come for you. At the last minute he couldn't get away. . . . I'm sorry."

"Don't apologize for him," said Laura. But she felt like grabbing a kitchen chair and throwing it through the window. A hotness was in her throat, a heavy clotting of tears or mucus, and she could hardly breathe. "Did you drive the car? Am I still supposed to bring everything?"

Leo walked to the sink and took a glass of water. He blotted his face with a paper towel. "No, your father'll come back some other time to close up the house. He said to just leave everything downstairs."

"I better go," said Gabrielle.

"I'll be right back," said Laura. She walked Gabrielle to the front door. "Maybe sometime you and Greg could drive to New York and we could go out. I keep telling you— it's not that far, only two and a half hours."

"Sure," said Gabrielle and stepped onto the path. Every summer, they'd talked about Gabrielle coming for a visit, but it had never happened.

"I mean it. . . . I really want to see you. I don't know if I'm coming back to Ventnor or not." Laura was yelling now because Gabrielle was walking away, up Marion Avenue to catch the bus. "I'm sorry," she yelled. "Good-bye, good-bye."

She went to the curb and looked up and down the street, but Gabrielle had already turned the corner. There was no one on the sidewalk, no cars cruising slowly by. The sky was hot and sunny, without a cloud. Laura let her shoulders drop and suddenly realized she was no longer afraid.

In the kitchen Leo was putting the dishes in the dishwasher away. "You don't have to do that," Laura told him. "When are we leaving?"

"The next helicopter is at five-thirty."

"Can you do me a favor, Leo?"

"Anything." He put the last cups into the cabinets, then turned to her and smiled.

"If we take the helicopter, we'll pass right by Trump's . . ."

"And you want me to go into the casino and get Billy for you."

"How did you know that?" asked Laura, amazed.

"He doesn't know you're leaving today, right? If it were me, I'd certainly want to say good-bye to him. That was his sister who was here, wasn't it?"

Laura put her palm on her forehead. "God, I never even introduced you!"

"That's okay," said Leo. "I figured it out. Now hurry up and get whatever you want to take with you. How about if I tell the car service to come in fifteen minutes?"

"I'll be ready."

Laura sat on one of the benches on the boardwalk, looking out to sea. The beach was jammed as usual, and the brightly colored cloth cabanas the hotels used for guests billowed in the wind. The sound of the waves was soothing, muffling everything.

"Laura?" Billy sat next to her and took her hand. He looked sorrowful, but the gold threads in his dealer's uniform glittered gaily in the sunshine.

"Where's Leo?"

"He'll be back in a few minutes. He said he was going to get something to eat."

"I'm glad he could find you."

"Yeah. It worked out well. I was just about to go on my break."

Laura leaned against Billy. She felt his heart speed up and she turned and slipped her hand underneath his vest, searching for the heartbeat. "Ah, there it is. I'm glad you like me so much. Will you come to New York to visit me sometime?"

"Is tomorrow too soon?"

She drew back to look at him, to see if he was serious.

"I'm kidding. But sure, yes. I want to see you. I've never even been to New York."

"But it's so close . . ."

"So are Baltimore and Philly. And Washington, D.C.," said Billy. He slipped between the bars of the boardwalk railing. "Come on, let's walk down to the water."

"What about Leo?"

"I told him we'd meet him at five-fifteen at the helicopter landing."

Nobody was swimming on this part of the beach. An old man was wading with his pants rolled up and a few children were playing tag, their cries drowned out by the surf. Down at the edge of the ocean, Billy and Laura could have been in a room alone.

For a long time they did not speak. When Laura turned to look at Billy, he was staring at her so hard, she had the feeling he was trying to memorize her face. "I don't like that. Don't look at me that way. Please."

"Why not? What's wrong with looking? I haven't touched you, have I?" He moved away from her a little and took off his shoes and socks. "I saw your friend the blackjack player this afternoon," he said, straightening.

"What do you mean?"

"You heard me. He was at my table a half-hour ago. Placing some big bets, too. My friend pointed him out to me, but as it turns out I already knew him. Ari Hassan. He's one of those who lives for the tables. You never said it was Ari Hassan."

"It isn't. I don't know what you're talking about."

"Oh, really? Well, how about if I go back and ask him about you? He'll probably still be playing after the break . . . if he has any money left. Last weekend my friend told me he dropped twenty thousand dollars."

Laura grabbed Billy's arm. "Don't do that," she pleaded. "Don't say anything about me."

"Jesus, Laura. I was only kidding." He put his arms

around her and held her tightly. "What did the guy do to you, anyway?"

"Nothing really. Please. Let's just forget it."

Two little girls and their mother settled down on the sand nearby with a beach umbrella and pails and shovels. Suddenly Laura knew she had to get out of here. She tried to focus on New York, but instead she imagined Leo in his rumpled suit, waiting with her suitcase at the helicopter landing.

"It must be almost time to leave. Isn't it close to five-fifteen? I better go. I still have to walk a long way to meet Leo."

"I wish I could go with you," said Billy. "But I have to get back. I hate my job. Did I ever tell you that? I might go to college this fall, maybe at Stockton."

"I hope you do it. That would be great."

They climbed up on the boardwalk and Laura sat with Billy as he brushed the sand off his feet and put his shoes and socks back on. She took a pen out of her purse and ripped a page from her checkbook ledger. "Here's my phone number in New York. It's at Heather and Leo's in Brooklyn. I'm going to be staying with them for a while."

"I won't ever say anything to Ari Hassan, Laura. I swear it."

"I believe you," said Laura. She went up to Billy so that their bodies were touching all along their lengths. "Thank you for everything this summer."

"I'll miss you," said Billy.

"Yes, I know." She waved at him and watched him walk away, backward down the boardwalk.

"I've already said good-bye too many times today. I can't take it," Laura said.

She and Leo were standing outside the chain-link fence at the helicopter landing, waiting to board. The black Trump helicopter had arrived and was on the ground with its hatch open and its propeller whirling while two mechanics in blue jumpsuits checked it over.

"You don't have to say good-bye to me," said Leo.

"True." Laura remembered the first time she'd seen Leo. She'd had no way to think about a person like him besides the outward impression his looks had made. But now his steadiness stayed with her.

While they'd been waiting, a line of other passengers had formed behind them. Everyone was yelling because the helicopter was a half-hour late leaving, but finally a stewardess marched past and led them beneath the hot diesel breath of the propeller and up the helicopter's steps.

Leo said, "Take a window seat on the left. Then you'll be able to see us go through the span on the Verrazano Narrows Bridge."

They were still on the ground and all Laura saw was the asphalt lot and the two mechanics talking. She thought one of them might be the man who'd yelled at her and chased her away when she was trying to eat her lunch on the landing, but it was hard to be sure.

A recorded voice came over the loudspeakers, giving instructions about what to do in case of an emergency landing. Laura tried to listen but the helicopter was lifting up, straight up into the sky. She hadn't wanted to ever fly again. She'd sworn she wouldn't, and yet here she was.

She closed her eyes and put her head back, feeling the vibrations of the engine pour through her body. Next to her Leo was opening a magazine. The stewardess handed Laura a package of sugared peanuts and asked what she wanted to drink. Finally Laura looked down.

Atlantic City was nothing—a few tall buildings huddled on a beach. Marshes and bays surrounded it and the Atlantic Ocean stretched endlessly to the east, a vast and watery world. The fish were swimming in the sea and the gulls were perched on the water in flocks, bobbing up and down.

"How are you doing?" asked Leo.

"I'm happy," said Laura.